The kelp, twenty-eight feet tall, as impressive in its own way as a stand of redwoods, began to sway. Water swirled as if a wave had hit, which is what the surge simulates, and an object caught in the forest worked its way loose. It looked like a gray jacket, windbreaker-style, with a red splatter on it. Another foreign object floated gracefully toward the bottom—a woman's high heel. Automatically, I looked up.

The body of a woman floated on top of the kelp canopy. I stared, transfixed, at a leopard shark shaking its body, its teeth caught in the woman's panty hose. Something nasty was sticking out of the woman's eye; it looked like the ivory handle of a fancy knife.

Also by Julie Smith:

HUCKLEBERRY FIEND
TOURIST TRAP
TRUE-LIFE ADVENTURE
THE SOURDOUGH WARS
DEATH TURNS A TRICK
NEW ORLEANS MOURNING*

Published by Ivy Books

DEAD
IN THE
WATER

Julie Smith

IVY BOOKS • NEW YORK

Ivy Books
Published by Ballantine Books
Copyright © 1991 by Julie Smith

Library of Congress Catalog Card Number: 91-92204

ISBN-0-8041-0855-2

Manufactured in the United States of America

First Edition: Decmeber 1991

For Aliza P. Rood, a friend of the sea otter

It was one of those days in Monterey when the air is washed and polished like a lens. The sunshine had a goldy look and the red geraniums burned the air around them. The delphiniums were like little openings in the sky. There aren't many days like that anyplace.

John Steinback, *Sweet Thursday*

Acknowledgments

The Monterey Bay Aquarium is a real and very wonderful place much as depicted herein except for one tiny detail—it's staffed by perfectly lovely people (not a murderer in the bunch), many of whom contributed to this book not only with generosity but with joy and gusto. I particularly want to thank Judy Rand, as knowledgeable and delightful a guide as anyone could have, and her colleagues, Steve Downey and John O'Sullivan. Need I mention that none of the characters are based on them or anyone else who works at the aquarium or ever has? Lieutenant Ken Brown of the Monterey Police Department, Christina Parsons, Dr. Patty Barnwell, and Frank Clark were equally generous with their time and expertise. Kit Tomas explained about certain saltwater treasures, and no less than three lawyers offered opinions about the best way to handle the case. My thanks to James Crowder, Michael Ganschow, and Carolyn Wheat for not charging by the hour.

CHAPTER 1

Sometimes in the life of a lawyer (even one as dedicated as I), there comes an overpowering urge to be under the sea, not so much in an octopus's garden as in a hermit crab's.

I indulge this fantasy vicariously, by keeping a one-hundred-gallon saltwater aquarium in my living room. A lot of people think I'm weird.

Marty Whitehead was weird, too.

It was late August when she called that last time, and I was staring out my office window thinking how odd it was to feel so empty and sad on such a beautiful day. I didn't want to make nice over lunch. I wanted to hole up like a hermit and be as crabby as I liked.

"Gosh-I'd-love-to, so-sorry, I'm-booked," I said, or something close enough. I'd said it a lot lately and I was getting it down pat.

"Drinks then?"

"I'd really love to, but I've got to try this case tomorrow and I could probably be ready sometime in October if I worked every minute. One of those things, maybe next time . . ."

"Oh." Her voice was low and gave nothing away, but something didn't feel right.

"Marty, is anything wrong?"

"No, I'm fine. Well, I guess you should know, but it's all

1

right, I'm coping just fine. Don's dumped me, but it's okay. Really."

Rob Burns hadn't dumped me, exactly, but it was our relationship that had me in the dumps, and you know what they say about misery. I had the damn drink with her.

My true love had gotten a Nieman Fellowship and had already left for Cambridge to find an apartment. I knew that Nieman Fellows returned from Harvard after a year; and that, like anyone else in this great country, they were free to receive visitors during their year. And I knew that a Nieman was about as prestigious as anything in journalism and that this was the high point of Rob's career. So why was I so sad?

Because I knew it was over, that's why. Rob didn't know, but I did. I wasn't sure what the problem was, exactly. The easy explanation was that I felt he cared more about his job than he did about me. He was a reporter for the *Chronicle*— a workaholic who could forget dates and cancel weekends when he was on a good story. But I had a nagging feeling that was only an explanation of convenience.

There was my half to think about, too. I found myself more and more haunted by ugly questions, questions like "What's wrong with me?" Or worse: "Am I really so unlovable, his job looks better?"

Since I like to think of myself as an independent, capable, twenty-first-century kind of woman, these clingy thoughts, so suggestive of poor self-esteem and emotional dependency, weren't comfortable, to say the least—even buried deep, which was where I carried them. You bet I kept them deep. No Rob Burns or anybody else was going to view the spectacle of Rebecca Schwartz begging and nagging.

After two years of the same old setup, I had to conclude that, for whatever reason—something about me, something about him, something about both of us—Rob wasn't really working out.

It was going to be an awful wrench. If anything, the Nieman made the whole thing easier, because he'd be gone in a natural way while I got used to the idea—but not having him around was going to be hard as hell. It already was. He'd only been gone a week and I was moping about so unproductively that Chris Nicholson, my law partner, was begging me to take a vacation and make it official. My sister Mickey, able to tell by my eyebags how badly I was sleeping, had shown her concern by giving me some Seconal prescribed for her after a miscarriage.

Our smart-aleck secretary, Alan Kruzick, had hung the office in black the day before Marty called—you'd have thought it was someone's fortieth birthday. Kruzick, one of The King's most loyal subjects, had an Elvis song for every occasion and a blaster to play it on. His favorite trick was to greet me with the song of the day, flipping the switch when I walked in. The day of the black office, it was "Heartbreak Hotel." Normally I would simply have picked up the nearest chair and heaved it at him. That day I broke into tears.

So I was easy prey for Marty. She was someone who'd be so busy crying in her own beer, she wouldn't mind if I did the same. In fact, she was so much worse off than I was that I could almost forget my own troubles. I didn't for an instant buy that "really okay" garbage.

We'd met at a party. "Marty," said our host, "has an aquarium even bigger than yours."

"Saltwater?" I'd asked her.

"Uh-huh."

Already I liked this woman. Saltwater aquariums are much rarer and tougher to maintain than freshwater ones. "How many gallons?"

"Let's see. Nearly three-quarters of a million, I think—if you count all three tanks."

Our host, I saw, had been putting me on. This was no

living room fishbowl we were speaking of. "You must live in Monterey," I said.

"Yes. I'm marketing director at the aquarium."

The Monterey Bay Aquarium is one of the wonders of the world. I was momentarily filled with envy.

"How marvelous!" I blurted. "And how are 'the lovely animals of the sea, the sponges, tunicates, anemones, the stars and buttlestars, and sun stars—' "

Marty took up the quote " '—the bivalves, barnacles, the worms and shells, the fabulous and multiform little brothers—' " She stopped, looking exhausted. "And so on. My favorites are the anemones." Mine, too—Marty was making big points, but she didn't even stop for air. "You should see what we got this week—a wonderful, funny Mola mola. It's so ugly, you want to take it home and kiss it."

"But molas are open-ocean fish."

She shrugged happily. "Now and then they wander into the bay, looking a little like bewildered Frisbees."

Pleased with himself, if a little mixed-up, our host had drifted on, knowing he'd delighted a couple of aliens who'd found someone with whom to speak their native tongue.

Marty and I could have gone on about bivalves and barnacles for hours (and did for the better part of one), but our respective escorts eventually caught up with us—Rob and Marty's husband, Don.

When the gents turned up, the conversation swung, as it often did when Rob made a new acquaintance, to why the *Chronicle* was such a bad newspaper. Since Rob thought it quite a good paper and adored working there, it might be imagined this was not his favorite subject. But he was infinitely good-natured about it, and even persuasive as to his own view. And so he and Don hit it off as well.

The four of us went to dinner after the party, and Marty and Don swore to have us down to Monterey for a weekend. But Don was always traveling, it seemed. . . . Anyway, it never happened. On the other hand, Marty and I usually got together for lunch or drinks whenever she was in the city.

Now she had a dead marriage and two children—ages ten and twelve—who were sure to be as brokenhearted as she was. If you thought of the marriage as a fifteen-year investment, she also had fifteen years down the tube.

As we drank—she had white wine (quite a few glasses of it), I had red—I got the whole story, probably now in its hundred-and-ninth telling: "It was so *sudden*, Rebecca. There was no way to see it coming, no way to prepare.

"One day he came home and said we had to talk. I'd gotten off early and I was making vegetable soup. He said he'd fallen in love with somebody else and he was moving out." She shrugged. "And that was that."

"Pretty much of a shock."

"The shock was the worst part." She straightened her spine and stared straight ahead. "But I'm over it now."

Sure she was.

Not knowing what to say, I let some time go by, thinking I was witnessing one of the worst cases of denial I'd seen. I've noticed some people cover their sadness with rage, and some, their rage with denial. Marty seemed to be in the latter class, but she'd at least gotten down to rage in one area. She said in a voice loud enough for everyone in Tosca to hear, "He didn't even tell me who she was!"

"It was someone you knew?"

"My boss."

Marty had a one-of-a-kind job. The family had moved to Monterey on her account, not Don's. She might be in marketing—the least piscine of jobs at the aquarium—but she could be in marketing anywhere. She was there because she loved the sea and its wildly teeming life. She was as dedicated to that aquarium as if it were in her living room. You didn't just walk away from a job like hers. But how could you work with a boss who had committed grand larceny in your bed?

"Sadie Stoop-Low," said Marty, draining her glass (and listing a little, I thought).

"I beg your pardon?"

"Swedlow. Sadie Swedlow in the phone book. Bitch!"

Her sibilants were getting slushy. Some people feed their denial with alcohol. Starting to worry, I said, "You aren't driving back tonight, are you?"

"Sure, why not?"

I devoted the next half hour to talking her out of it, five minutes to phoning her sitter, and the hour after that to nursemaid services involving more drinking and more listening. It was almost midnight before I got her bedded down in my living room, an eminently soothing place for a fish-fancier.

She awoke fresh and grateful, but a little sheepish. "Gosh, Rebecca, I don't usually drink that much."

"Marty, listen, something awful's happened to you. You have a right to drown your sorrows."

"It wasn't that. I'm coping fine. I should have had more than a salad for dinner, that's all. I've gained two pounds in the last month, and I've got to take it off."

"You're such a perfectionist. Did it ever occur to you that you're as human as anyone else? You just lost your husband of fifteen years. You're allowed to feel terrible about it."

She looked at her watch and screwed up her lip, irritated, letting me see what she was thinking: How dare I talk to her this way? We weren't really that close. Even the night before, even in the face of disaster, she hadn't really unbuttoned, just vented steam about Sadie.

"Well, listen," she said. "Whatever. The point is, you saved my life and put me up, and I'd love to return the hospitality. You're the one who's going through a bad time. Look at you. Your face is so tense, it looks like a mask. You need to get out of here for a while. So get your things. We're going to Monterey.''

I almost smiled, she was so transparent—trying to reassure herself by taking control. But she'd hit on something. It was all I could do not to dash for my toothbrush.

I really did have to be in court or I would have taken her up on the offer right then. The moment she brought up the idea, I knew Monterey was the place I needed to be. If I found my own aquarium healing, what about the biggest one in the world? *I must go down to the sea again*, said some silly imp who lives in my brain, and I actually smiled.

She saw the smile and zeroed in for the kill. ''You know what we have in Monterey now? This thing called The American Tin Cannery—outlet heaven.''

Everyone who knows me knows I love to shop and I love a bargain.

Marty said, as if dangling cookies before a kid, ''There's a Joan and David outlet.''

But I wasn't even slightly moved. It was the aquarium that attracted me, and the bay.

If I couldn't actually be a hermit crab, at least I could imitate one, and I could look at quite a few. I could watch the kelp forest sway all day if I wanted to, and I could sit in the restaurant at the aquarium and eat delicious seafood and drink the amusingly named house Chardonnay (Great White) and watch the bay. I would see seals and otters, perhaps, and if I didn't, I could take a cruise on the bay. I could reread *Cannery Row*.

The only things wrong with this picture were Marty and her two kids. Hermit crabs have to have solitude.

But eventually we worked it out. Chris was already prepared to take over my cases if only I'd get out of the office for a while. I'd drive down that night, which was Friday, spend the weekend at Marty's, and find a nice condo or B&B to move into on Monday—something on the beach, maybe, or at least within walking distance of the aquarium. And I'd stay there a week, two weeks, maybe three. I'd stay there till I felt better.

CHAPTER 2

Cannery Row is a colorful old street, once called Ocean View. To its biographer, John Steinbeck, it was "a poem, a stink, a grating noise, a quality of light, a tone, a habit, a nostalgia, a dream."

Steinbeck's book was published in 1945, the best year ever for the sardine catch, and for practical purposes, the last good year. The last cannery, the Hovden (which produced the Portola brand sardine), closed in 1952.

And so nowadays the stink is largely metaphorical, the latter-day fishiness having to do with authenticity or the lack of it, for Cannery Row is now tourist-land, a street of restaurants, hotels, bars, T-shirt shops, and one cultural attraction.

Oddly, the rest of Steinbeck's description more or less holds true. The row is right on the bay, you can't change that—and it's still got its own unique, half-industrial character. The aquarium, tucked in at the end of the row, the old "Portola" sign meticulously preserved on its adjoining warehouse wall, is the one cultural attraction.

As we'd arranged, I phoned Marty when I got into town. She was working late, which seemed odd for a Friday, but she said she was catching up after her two days in San Francisco. She said she'd meet me in the parking lot, where we could leave my car while we had dinner at some splendid fish place. (People who love aquatic animals love them in every way.)

She had me park in the dirt lot on what is still Ocean View Boulevard, but becomes Cannery Row at the Monterey line—weirdly, the aquarium is on the border of Pacific Grove and Monterey. When I got out of the car, she gave me a big hug as if we were best friends instead of fairly distant acquaintances, and I started getting into the holiday aspect of the thing. She led me through the gate to the closer, paved parking lot, both of us chattering as if we hadn't seen each other in months instead of hours.

She seemed much cheerier than she'd been in the city. That was the way these things went, I remembered from my last breakup. You were morbidly depressed for a while, and then you started having some good days, and eventually most days were pretty good. Don had been gone three months.

"Are the kids coming to dinner with us?" I asked.

"Oh, heavens no. They're in front of the tube and can't be pried away. Keil's twelve, you know, and very responsible. Damn good businessman, too—takes after his mom. He has his own errand-running business, called Trap Door, Ltd. It's not really a limited partnership, of course." She sounded like the Stanford M.B.A. she was. "The 'limited' part refers to the way he feels, not having a driver's license—has to work on a bike, poor baby."

"What does the Trap Door part mean?"

"You don't get it?"

"Not offhand."

"He's got a wild imagination, I guess." She sighed, as if this were not a good thing. "If you get in a bind, and can't get your chores done, you can escape via Trap Door."

"Ah. Pretty clever."

"He also baby-sits, which is what he's doing tonight. Of course, he charges more for it than any kid in the neighborhood, but he's worth it—the first time he sits, he reels off the phone numbers of the police and fire departments, demonstrates the Heimlich maneuver, and assures you he knows CPR in case your kid—in this case, your other kid—has a heart attack. The boy loves his money. Anyway, not everyone wants to baby-sit Libby. Especially since Don left.''

''Why not?''

''She's—ah—difficult.''

Terrific. I'd just signed up to spend the weekend with the Bad Seed.

''Rebecca, I've got a surprise for you before we eat. Have you ever seen a kelp forest at night?''

''We're going to look at the aquarium? I thought we were getting your car.''

Marty smiled enigmatically. She wasn't the sort you usually think of as having a flair for drama. She was short, with dirty-blond hair, brown eyes, and light skin with a dusting of freckles. Her hair was naturally wavy, and though she obviously had it cut professionally, she'd opted for neatness rather than style—if asked how she wore it, I would have had to say ''on her head.'' Nothing else really came to mind.

Her features were neat and ordinary as well, and so was her businesswoman's gym-trained figure. The only remarkable thing about Marty seemed to be her love of the ocean. Unless she had her own hidden depths.

''Is this legal? To go in at night?'' I said, hoping it wasn't.

''Oh, perfectly. It's a great place for night parties. In fact, arranging them is one of the things we do in marketing. There isn't one tonight, though.'' She dropped her voice to a whisper. ''It'll be quiet as the grave.''

''That should suit our mood.''

''Oh, cheer up—that's the point of all this.'' She snapped her fingers. ''I know what you'll like. Let's go see the mola first. It's in quarantine.''

She turned left, toward an outside shedlike affair. ''This is aquarist territory.''

"And aquarists are?"

"The husbandry people. They're all marine biologists, they're all divers, and I think all of them at least have their master's. Very, very well qualified. And they live the sea. When they're not diving, they're sailing, and when they're not sailing, they're eating sushi. Look, there are the 'thermal recovery units.' "

"The what?"

She laughed. "Hot tubs. But they really do need them. It's sixty degrees in the bay. You can get hypothermia so fast it's scary."

The mola, lying on the surface of its tank, had lost its bewildered look, but it was as Frisbee-like as ever. Also known as the ocean sunfish, it must be named for its shape, but the nickname seems far too bright and cheerful for so grotesque a creature. As a matter of fact, I bow to no one in my fanship of molas; they're utterly fascinating beasts. But the phrase "monster of the deep" does rather come to mind at first sight of one. The mola has the misfortune to look like half a fish. It's not completely flat, but close enough. It looks something like a frying pan with arms.

"Marty, that thing's weird."

"I knew you'd love it. They're warm-water fish—that's why we can't keep them in the tanks. Relatives of the puffer; you probably know that."

"You mean the dread fugu?"

"Uh-huh. We have a couple of those, too—upstairs in our Sea of Cortez exhibit. Want to see?"

"No, thanks. They give me the creeps."

When I had admired the evolutionary accident to her satisfaction, Marty took me into the building itself, through a back entrance that seemingly opened into a labyrinth—and we still weren't even in the aquarium.

"This is the old Hovden warehouse; you know that, right? Its office space connects with the aquarium proper—I'm on the third floor. Here are the aquarists' offices, and our library, and the volunteer office. We have about five hundred fifty volunteers, can you believe it? Here's the volunteer and staff lounge, there's an exhibits area, and here's a little back room where they do graphics.''

She gave me a proprietary smile. ''A lot of people work here. It takes a staff of two hundred seventy full- and part-time people to run this place, in addition to the volunteers. Oh, and another fifty in the restaurant.''

I had a sudden flash of envy—she was so much at home here. ''I wish I'd been a marine biologist,'' I said. ''Instead of a lawyer.''

Marty laughed, secure in her own place, husband-stealing boss or no, and opened a door to the aquarium-behind-the-scenes, a place of wet floors and another kind of labyrinth. ''The exhibit area is in the heart of the place, but it's surrounded by all this.'' She gestured. ''Actually, there's almost as much of this space as there is exhibit area. Come on—I'll show you where the aquarists work, and how they go into the tanks.''

I followed silently.

''They took a lot of care with this building,'' she said, ''in just about every way you can think of. Because it's on the site of the old Hovden Cannery, it's built to resemble the Hovden as much as possible.'' She pointed, continuing the tour. ''There's the freight elevator—it goes up to the roof. And here—'' she opened a door ''—is what we call a service area. This is where the aquarists work.''

There were more wet, slippery floors here, and pipes and things you could hit your head on. Fiberglass platforms surrounded the tanks, which were ordinary white vessels on three sides, but windowed on the fourth. Inside were small exhibits. From where we were, you could look down into the tank, and feed the fish if you were an aquarist. The view was ordinary. But from the window out front, it was a stunning vista.

For the first time, I started to understand the showmanship that had gone into the design of the place.

Some of it, indeed, was done with mirrors. Marty pointed one out. "See that? With the cloud of blue rockfish? From the front, it looks like a sand channel, opening back to more and more blue rockfish.

"And these are called 'inserts,' " she said, noting the lining of one of the tanks. "They're slabs of fake rock that have been in the bay a while, growing things. Oh, look at this." She plucked a tiny starfish from behind the insert and put him back on exhibit.

I was staring at pale pink anemones, thinking of the vicious 'clone wars' these pretty things fight, when Marty shrieked, "Would you look at the size of this melibe!"

Behind me, I stared into a tank that wasn't on exhibit. The melibe—or sea slug—was something like a giant, nearly transparent Venus's-fly-trap, and looked like a parachute. It was about two feet long, which must be long for a melibe.

"These things smell great," she said. "Like melon, although I don't know if that's where the name comes from. We'll get an aquarist to take one out for you one day—they look like a little pile of Jell-O when you put them on your palm."

I was impatient. "Let's go see the kelp tank."

We stepped into the exhibit area.

The Monterey Bay Aquarium is very different indeed from other aquariums, which are basically collections of fish from around the world, especially the tropics. This one shows you what you'd see if you were a hermit crab living in the bay, which itself is not just any bay. As anyone knows who's read *Cannery Row*, it teems with darting, swirling, multicolored, many-shaped life. Even when you know that, it's quite a bit more than you could possibly imagine it is, standing on the shore and looking out. Underneath it, stretching sixty miles out to sea, and two miles down at its seaward end, is Monterey Canyon, as large and deep as the Grand Canyon.

So that's the bay. Its many habitats, from the deep reefs to the wharf, are re-created within the aquarium, in panoramic vistas that make your breath catch—far, far, from the old-fashioned window-in-the-wall approach. The most famous of the exhibits is the towering kelp forest, three stories high, sixty-six feet long, containing 335,000 gallons of water, its seven-inch-think acrylic walls made in Japan by a secret process and assembled on Cannery Row by experts who forbade aquarium officials to watch. It is the tallest aquarium exhibit in the world, and arguably the most spectacular.

"Damn!"

"What is it?"

"The lights are off."

The kelp forest was dark.

"The lights are on the roof. They usually have them on for night parties," said Marty. "I forgot they might be off. Tell you what we'll do—we'll call the control room and get them turned on. The surge machine, too."

We walked down the stairs to the first floor, where there's a little gallery in front of the kelp forest. Here the floor is carpeted, and there are a few stair-step benches where you can sit in case you become mesmerized and unable to move.

Marty left me and went to the information desk to use the phone. In a moment, the lights lit the tank, as if the house lights had gone up on a stage. A big gold garibaldi darted away, startled. A sea cucumber, spiny and, to tell you the truth, somewhat revolting, had pasted itself to the far wall. Leopard sharks glided by, and thin, black-tailed senoritas. A rockfish, looking baleful, flapped its pectoral fins like wings. I was staring back at it, wondering if it was trying to make friends (and knowing better), when the surge machine went on.

The kelp, twenty-eight feet tall, as impressive in its own

way as a stand of redwoods, began to sway. Water swirled as if a wave had hit, which is what the surge simulates, and an object caught in the forest worked its way loose. It looked like a gray jacket, windbreaker-style, with a red splatter on it. Another foreign object floated gracefully toward the bottom—a woman's high heel. Automatically, I looked up.

The body of a woman floated on top of the kelp canopy. She was wearing a black business suit, which looked as if it was made of linen. I stared, transfixed, at a leopard shark shaking its body, its teeth caught in the woman's panty hose. Silver sardines swam under the body, and suddenly something yellow darted into the water, and one of the sardines flowed red.

The body changed position and surged downward for a moment so that I could see its face, black hair wreathing it eerily, like Medusa's. Something nasty was sticking out of the woman's eye; it looked like the ivory handle of a fancy knife.

Again, fast as a cat's paw, a pair of yellow pincers, now at the woman's neck, plunged toward a fish, this time missing. And another, at the waist. They were beaks.

I realized, knees starting to shake, that there were gulls standing on top of the body, fishing.

CHAPTER 3

"Marty!"

But she'd already seen it. She was making little noises like someone having a dream, trying to wake up. Her body was shaking. I took her shoulders and spoke softly. "It's okay, Marty. You're okay, we'll call security. Here—I'll help you sit down."

I pushed gently on her shoulders, trying to get her to sit on one of the benches, but she resisted. "It's Sadie," she whispered.

"Sadie Swedlow," I said, to show I understood.

She nodded.

"Okay. It's not you—it's not me. It's Sadie Swedlow."

"Rebecca!" Her teeth were chattering. "Look at that thing! That thing in her eye—"

"Yes. Someone stabbed her. It's okay. You're okay."

"Look at it!"

"Marty. We've got to call security." I spoke brusquely. I was through being soothing; it wasn't working anyway. She rallied enough to give me the number.

When I got back from the information desk, Marty had finally sat down, but she was still shivering. I took off my linen blazer and tried to tuck it around her. "My jacket," she said.

"Yes. You can have it for now."

She raised her hands, maybe meaning to point, but not

17

succeeding. Her hands fluttered and circled helplessly. And then she pulled herself up from the bottom of her spine, took a deep breath, and spoke coherently. "That's my jacket in there."

"The gray one? Floating?"

Two guards came. One helped me to get Marty to lie down with her feet elevated, and the other called the police. The young officer who arrived first looked twenty-five and reacted about like Marty. But a few minutes later, the place was crowded—and not only with Monterey's finest. The night staff crawled out of the woodwork—cleaning workers, late-working aquarists, another guard, and some people in business clothes, maybe from accounting or education. Firemen and paramedics arrived.

"Rebecca . . ." She was whispering again.

"Yes?"

"Did you see that thing in her eye?"

I nodded, wondering what else I could do to calm her—so far as I could see, no one had a pocket flask.

"I mean, did you get a really good look at it?"

"No. I looked away. I guess you did, too."

"I think it's my letter opener."

My mind went into gear, finally. Her jacket. And now her letter opener. And Sadie had just made off with her husband. I talked fast.

"Marty, I'm your lawyer. For right now, anyway. You can call someone else when they give you a chance, but—"

"No. I want you."

"Okay. Now, listen. Don't say a word to the police. Nothing. Except that I'm your lawyer and I've advised you not to talk. Not a word. Understand?"

She nodded, looking dazed, and I went to make a phone call I wished I'd already made.

I returned to Marty and knelt, about to reiterate the importance of clamming up. "Excuse me," said someone behind us. "I'm Paula Jacobson from the police department. This is Lloyd Tillman, Detective Lloyd Tillman, I should say. We understand you're the two who called security.

I stood up. "Rebecca Schwartz."

Slowly, Marty got up as well. "Marty Whitehead. Is she dead, Officer?"

Jacobson smiled. "It's 'Sergeant,' technically. But why don't you call me Paula? Maybe we could talk a few minutes while Detective Tillman and Ms. Schwartz—"

I broke the news. "I'm Ms. Whitehead's attorney and I've advised her not to talk to you. Could we have a few minutes alone, please?"

Jacobson raised an inquisitive eyebrow. She was tall and striking, someone who wanted to be noticed. But right now she was dressed carelessly in jeans, T-shirt, and white cotton blazer, as if she'd been home doing dishes when she got the call and had rushed out, grabbing the jacket on the fly.

"All right." But there was an angry edge to her voice.

She was probably in her early thirties. She had longish white-blond hair, split on the ends, black roots showing, olive skin, a long face, and eyebrows plucked to a thin line. A sad look in her dark eyes went with the longish face. Her thighs were mighty; I hadn't seen it yet, but I was willing to bet her backside matched. A strapping female, and I didn't trust that sad look she had. Depressed people can turn aggressive.

Tillman didn't look much like Mr. Nice Guy himself. He was beefy, even a little porky, a few years older than Jacobson, and he had one of those short, neat beards with no mustache. He hadn't said a word yet, but his scowl said not to mess with him. I wished we had a choice.

"Is she dead?" Marty asked again.

"Who, Marty?" asked Tillman.

"The woman in the tank."

He shrugged. "Who is she?"

"We were wondering that, too," I said quickly, hearing an "S" hiss out of Marty.

"You have no idea?"

Marty held her tongue. Good.

Jacobson smiled. "We don't know if she's dead. They haven't got her out of the tank yet."

Marty said, "I see." She was making a nice recovery.

I led Marty away and sat her on one of the benches. We had to whisper, but too bad—there were some things I had to cover. Fast. "Marty, what's going on here?"

"I didn't kill her."

"What else do I need to know?"

She shrugged. "I don't know what you mean."

"There's a good chance you could be arrested tonight."

Finally, as the light dawned, she began to look alarmed. "Me? For what?"

"Marty, you have a motive, and the weapon's yours. They don't need a lot more than that. What else is there? Did you and Sadie fight? Did you threaten her?"

"Of course not."

"Listen, Marty, I'm a good lawyer. I'll get you out of this if I can. But you have to help. I just called a bail bondsman in San Francisco—he's standing by, but I have to tell you— the cops'll call a judge and try to get him to let them hold you on a no-bail warrant. And there's a good chance they'll get it. Do you understand what I'm saying?"

She shook her head. How could she understand? "Marty, if they put you in jail tonight, you might not get out till Monday. All they need is probable cause, and they might think they have it. But our real problem is, it's Friday. You can't be arraigned till Monday. If a judge won't set bail, they can hold you till then."

"But this is America!"

I shrugged, having vented my spleen on this subject enough times. Defense lawyers like this rule of law the way we like black mambas, but there's nothing we can do about it. I didn't want to tell her, but they could actually hold her till Tuesday—the rule was seventy-two hours before she had to be arraigned, and weekends didn't count.

Marty got hold of herself. "But you can get me out on Monday?"

"Probably. But listen, Marty, you have to help me. Believe me, you don't want to go to jail. When did you last see Sadie?"

"I don't know—five o'clock maybe. Six. Who knows?"

"What time does the aquarium close?"

"Six."

"Where were you between six and the time I got here?"

"In my office. Working."

"Were other people there?"

"Are you kidding? It's Friday."

"Did Sadie leave at six with the others?"

"I don't know. I didn't see her."

"Did you see anyone in that period? Before I got here?"

"No."

My heart raced. If they decided to take her in, I didn't see what I could do about it.

Tillman came over. "Will *you* talk to us, Ms. Schwartz?"

"Certainly."

He sighed, and began the mechanical questions: When did I arrive? How did I get in? Did I go anywhere before coming into the kelp forest area? What did I see when I got here?

How did the lights happen to be on?

What time had it been when we called the control room?

What exactly did I see when the lights went on?

What else?

And on and on like that for several millennia. Similar scenes were being acted out around us with other employees,

as public servants of one sort or another—we certainly had
a variety on hand—fished out Sadie Swedlow.

Finally one of the other cops called Tillman away. I felt
like a boxer's corner man between rounds, and wished I had
his equipment—Marty needed her face wiped and maybe a
little water thrown in it.

We were alone again for a long while. Marty said, "Why
don't you want me to talk to them?"

"Surely you've heard the phrase 'Anything you say can
and will be used against you.' They're not kidding about
that."

"But if I'm not guilty, how can I incriminate myself?"

I winced, imagining about three hundred different ways.
To change the subject, I said, "Who else had a reason to kill
her?"

"The bitch! Anybody might have. She'd slept with half
the guys who work here. Miss Sadie Stoop-Low was certainly never troubled about scruples—she was the boss, and
she used it every way she could. Took what she wanted from
everybody else—everything from free overtime to sex—and
she was nasty."

"To whom?"

"To everybody except her favorites—needless to say, they
were all men."

"She wasn't popular?"

"She was a bitch."

"She must have been a good administrator, or she wouldn't
have lasted in a job like that."

"I doubt she would have lasted. She'd only been here six
months."

"She was pretty busy if she'd already alienated half the
staff and slept with the other half."

"That's our Sadie." There was real venom in her voice.

The cops came back. "Marty Whitehead," Jacobson said,

"you're under arrest." She proceeded to read Marty her rights.

I grabbed Tillman. "Are you crazy? You don't have any reason to arrest her. This is a woman with strong community ties—you can't afford to make a mistake."

He was smooth, I'll give him that. "Want to come up to the roof with me?"

We took the freight elevator, and when we got off, the first thing I saw was a body bag—Sadie, awaiting her ride to the morgue.

From this vantage point, the kelp forest looked like nothing more romantic than a swimming pool surrounded by a flimsy fence of plastic wire. The wire was attached to posts by hooks that could easily be removed, and some of them had been, to get the body out. The lights around the tank were giant, powerful ones—had to be to illuminate twenty-eight feet of murk—and near the surface swam the phosphorescent sardines, a habit they have that made them easy prey on moonless nights back in the cannery days. Even now, a sea gull dived at a silvery target.

The jacket I'd seen floating in the tank was lying on the floor.

"That's been identified as your client's. It's got blood all over it. Like maybe she wore it while she stabbed the victim. And I want to show you something else." He produced a plastic evidence bag, holding it so the contents could be very clearly seen. In the bag was a letter opener with a scrimshaw handle, the thing I'd seen sticking out of Sadie's face. Its steel point was almost blunt—a lot of force and a lot of brutal rage would be needed to shove it into a person.

"We hear her husband gave her this."

I could have said, "Estranged husband," just to set the record straight, but it wouldn't have been politic.

Tillman continued, "The body has been identified as that of Sadie Swedlow. We understand she was your client's boss.

One of the witnesses says they haven't been getting along lately. We hear her husband moved in with Sadie about three months ago. And we hear they had quite a fight about that time." He flipped some pages of his notebook. "We also hear she made a remark to the effect that she'd like to feed Ms. Swedlow to the sharks. And she was seen here tonight."

Terrific. Fights, threats, physical evidence, and placed at the scene. Why the hell hadn't she told me about the fight?

I said, "She 's got two little kids. She's not going anywhere."

He shrugged. He'd brought me up there to brag. He thought he had a pretty good case.

"All these witnesses you mentioned—did any of them see Marty with Sadie tonight?"

He was silent.

"With all due respect, Detective, you haven't got a damn thing."

Again, he shrugged. Why should he say anything? It was a one-sided argument, lost before it began.

I said, "I need to talk to her some more."

"Meet us at the station."

The police department was off Friendly Plaza, a small-town touch I liked. It was housed in an unimposing one-story building that could have been used for dentists' offices, it looked so innocuous, but I wondered what else was in there. Was there a jail, or were prisoners sent to a county institution?

We were ushered into a suffocating interview room, big enough for one person to breathe comfortably, but unfortunately there were two of us. Marty's face had turned as white as Jacobson's hair, and it wasn't much healthier-looking. The walls were covered with fake paneling, there were no windows except one to the room next door that was obviously a two-way, and the only furniture was a small table and two chairs covered with turquoise vinyl.

I was sure Marty had never been in such a place before. She swiveled her head continually, as if committing the whole place to memory, no doubt redecorating in her mind, removing the tacky paneling. Her nose seemed set in a permanent sniff. I didn't think she had a clue what kind of trouble she was in.

I told her what Tillman had told me.

"I didn't threaten her."

"You didn't say that about feeding her to the sharks?"

"That wasn't a threat! It was just one of those things you say."

I shrugged.

"Her little boyfriend must have told them that. Ricky Flynn."

"I thought Don was her boyfriend."

She blew her nose, leaving me with my mind on her husband.

"Where is he, by the way? Surely the police must have notified him. Will he do anything—" I searched for the right word" —inappropriate?"

I meant would he come to her house and make some kind of scene involving the kids—maybe say she was a murderer and try to haul them away. But Marty's thoughts were elsewhere. "Dear God, he's in Australia! Who'll take care of the kids?"

I guess I should have been glad she was being realistic, but the way she seemed to be accepting a weekend in jail made me worry: about her fighting spirit and about her innocence. It struck me suddenly that it was awfully convenient, my being there. I wondered if I'd been set up. But if Marty'd gone to so much trouble to get me in place for the big moment, why hadn't she bothered to arrange an alibi?

She tapped the table, thinking, still pale, but otherwise

cool. I was sure it was her ability to operate and plan under pressure that made her good in business, and it seemed to have kicked in. It was a little unnerving in this circumstance. "My mother. I'll get her to come down from Walnut Creek. But I'll need somebody tonight."

She raised her eyes to mine and simply stared. I'd known this was coming. If I didn't blink first, could I get out of it? I blinked. She kept staring.

"Marty, for Christ's sake. I don't even know your kids. A stranger's supposed to tell them their mother's in jail?"

I saw the tears pop into her eyes. "I don't have anybody else."

"Okay, okay. I'll do it."

She handed me her keys. "Here. Your room's the second one on the left at the top of the stairs."

"What time do they get up?"

She gave me an impatient wave, her mind already elsewhere. "Any time. Listen, there's one more thing. I need something from my office."

"You're going to work in jail? Are you crazy? Do you know how serious this is?"

"The police might search my office, right?"

"If they have reason to think there's evidence there. But there has to be probable cause for that, too, and they'd have to get a search warrant."

"I need my calendar."

"Your calendar?"

"And one other little thing. In one of my desk drawers— I don't know which, dammit—there's a note. It says, 'Six tonight?' or something like that. With a flowery phrase or two thrown in. I can't remember the exact wording, but you'll know it when you see it."

I was furious. So mad I practically stamped my feet. I didn't care if she was trying to protect the pope, I wasn't representing anyone stupid enough to play that game. Especially someone with two children who had to be told Mom was in jail. By me.

"Marty Whitehead, damn your eyes! Are you telling me you have an alibi?"

"How do I know, Rebecca? I don't know when she was killed."

"Common sense tells you she was killed after the aquarium closed. Between six and eight-thirty or thereabouts, when we found the body. Are you telling me you weren't even there at the time? You were with somebody who can give you an alibi?'

"No."

"Isn't that what you just told me?"

"I asked you to remove some personal things from my office, that's all—things I don't want the whole world to know about." She avoided my eyes, which probably looked like those of a hanging judge. "I was there tonight. My date was *last* Friday. Will you pick up my things, please? It's important to me."

They did have a jail in the building, and they got hold of a judge nasty enough to want to hold a mother of two without bail.

I had to leave alone, but I wasn't yet defeated. There was a chance—an outside chance, a tiny chance (actually an infinitesimal chance)—that sometime over the weekend I could find a judge who'd set bail.

CHAPTER
4

"Mommy! Mommy! Keil! Mommy's not home." Each word was shriller than the one before.

I rolled out of bed still groggy—keyed up from the excitement, I'd taken one of Mickey's Seconals. I grabbed a pair of shorts and pulled them on. I was already wearing panties and T-shirt, and I hadn't brought a robe.

"Libby? Libby, it's all right." I stumbled into the hall, where I smacked head-on into a ten-year-old juggernaut. Who would have thought such a small girl could seem so solid? She screamed; her eyes were terrified; trapped. Over her head, I saw the barrel of a rifle pointed at my heart. It was sticking out of one of the bedrooms, the door slightly cracked.

"Keil, it's okay, honey. I'm the sitter."

The gun barrel disappeared and Keil stepped out, still wearing pajamas. "It's only an air rifle." He was tall for his age, and handsome, blond with brown eyes. A surfer boy, a California dream.

Libby had plain brown hair, but she'd gotten blue eyes. Right now her teeth looked as big as a rabbit's, and they had a space between them. She was going through an awkward stage.

She screamed, "Where's my mom?"

"My name's Rebecca and I'm a friend of hers." I knelt down to make contact.

28

"Where is she?"

"She's all right. She's fine. I just—"

But Libby flounced away in midsentence. Keil said, "She's always like that."

I gave him a big smile. "I don't blame her. It must have been pretty upsetting waking up to find your mother gone."

"Ahhh—no big deal."

I thought he was working very hard to be brave. "Listen, Keil, I'm going to need some help. Could you get dressed and show me where things are in the kitchen? I'll make you some—uh—" What did kids like? "—French toast."

"Okay," he said, and went back to his room. Screams and wails were now coming from Libby's. I didn't know where to start.

I knocked on Keil's door. "Keil. Do you know how to make coffee? I think I'd better talk to Libby."

"Sure. I'll go make you some."

Libby was lying facedown on her bed, emitting high-volume screams. Keil came up behind me. "She's just trying to get attention."

Very well then, I'd give her some. "Libby, do you know who I am? Your mom's friend from San Francisco that likes fish?"

No answer. Gingerly I touched the small of her back. Her legs kicked out violently.

I said, "Honey, your grandmother's on the way—"

"I hate my grandmother!"

"How about breakfast? What do you think about breakfast?"

"I hate breakfast!"

And me? You hate me, too, right? I nearly had to bite my tongue to keep from saying it. "How about ice cream?"

"I hate ice cream!"

I walked to the door. "Too bad. I thought we'd have some for breakfast."

She turned around, her face pink and swollen. "I thought we were having French toast."

"We could—would you rather have that?"

She smashed her head down on the pillow again. "No!"

I went down to my coffee, which Keil, now in jeans, was just dripping into a mug that had a whale's fluke for a handle. He didn't waste a word. "Rebecca, where's Mom?"

"She's fine, Keil. Do you believe me?"

"If she's fine, why won't you tell me where she is?"

"I am going to tell you. I just don't want to do it twice. If you can get Libby to come down—"

Libby said, "I'm here," and padded in on bare feet, still in her nightgown. Hair hung over one eye, and, I had to admit it, she looked very cute.

"Aha! You came for French toast, did you?"

Keil said, "Tell us, Rebecca!" sounding as threatening as any street punk. I stared at him, shocked—he had seemed such a nice child. He looked half out of his mind with worry.

"Oh, Keil, I'm so sorry—I know you're very worried. Kids, your mom is fine, but something really bad has happened. She didn't do anything wrong—there was a terrible misunderstanding—but I'm afraid she had to spend the night in jail."

Libby's blue eyes widened into circles of sky.

Keil had recovered his composure. He rinsed the coffee funnel, making sure he kept his back elaborately turned. "What'd she do? Get in a brawl at a fern bar?"

"Keil. Libby. There's another piece of it." I paused, wondering if I really had to tell them, and concluding it wasn't right to keep it back. For all I knew, it was in the morning paper. "Something really, really bad has happened to Sadie Swedlow."

Fear, primitive, childish fear, the kind of fear you can only feel when you're a kid and things go out of control, filled Libby's eyes, contorted her face. "How bad?"

"Real bad, honey. She died last night."

Deep, wracking sobs erupted from her small body—not the angry, confused ones of a few moments ago. This was real sadness. I held out my arms to her and took a step forward, but she turned and ran. I realized I was crying myself. The back door slammed and I looked around, but Keil had left. I hadn't heard him move. I stood in the middle of the kitchen feeling miserable.

I hadn't been around kids much. I was shocked at how much of Libby's sadness I had picked up, and I thought I could feel Keil's, too. It was as if I'd gone suddenly psychic, lost the adult defenses it had taken me a lifetime to build. I took deep breaths, trying to figure out what was happening.

Were they so upset because they had loved Sadie? She hadn't been around long, but I was sure they'd been spending weekends, at least, with her and Don. There might have been time to build a rapport.

Or had they caught on that Sadie's death and their mother's being in jail were connected? Had it hit them in that millisecond that that had to be what their mom had been arrested for, and if so, how had they put it together so fast? Had they heard their mother threaten her? Or was it intuition?

In just a few minutes around these small beings, I was starting to understand that they lived in a different place from the one adults lived in, that they had transmitters and receivers that could get past normal barriers of communication. I don't mean I'd lived such an isolated life, I'd never seen a kid close up—far from it. But I hadn't been around them much under extreme stress, and I felt I'd just seen something naked and important. I thought that if I could tune in to where they were, I might learn something.

The next question, of course, was what to do next. Try to comfort Libby, probably, though I didn't think I'd get far. The doorbell rang as I started for the stairs.

"Oh." The caller was a gold-colored girl with black hair,

smaller than Libby, maybe a little younger. Looking confused, she turned briefly around as a silver-painted compact
drove away.

"It's okay. I'm Rebecca, the baby-sitter. Did you come to
see Libby?"

She nodded, looking very scared.

"Come in."

She did, but obviously because a grown-up was telling her
to, not because she wanted to. It was clear she wanted to run
for her life. Did I look weird?

It came to me that I hadn't combed my hair. I probably
had dreadlocks. I was going to have to fake being motherly—
it certainly didn't come natural. "What's your name, angel?
Would you like to sit down?"

"Esperanza." She made no move to sit.

"What a beautiful name. It's Spanish, isn't it?"

She looked anxiously at the stairs. "Honey, I'm not sure
Libby's going to be able to play this morning—let me just
ask her, shall I?"

She looked at me oddly. I thought she was wondering why
I didn't just send her up—she could ask Libby herself. I didn't
because I was afraid Libby in her current state would scare
her even worse. The girl would be sure I was holding Libby
captive and now had Esperanza to torture as well. Damn! If
only I could get to a comb—maybe she wouldn't be so nervous.

I raced up the stairs, not able to get away fast enough, and
found Libby crying her heart out. "Honey, Esperanza's
here."

No answer, just sobs.

"Shall I tell her you can't play?"

She nodded, the back of her head going up and down on
her pillow.

No surprises there. I ducked into a bathroom and saw that

I didn't look awful at all, but ran a comb through anyway and headed back down.

Esperanza was huddled small and miserable against a chair that would have held three of her, just leaning, not sitting down, as if at the ready for quick takeoff. "Sweetheart, I'm sorry, she just isn't up to it. Do you live close by?"

She shook her head.

I tried to think. I didn't want to leave Libby and Keil, assuming he was still somewhere about. For one thing, they hadn't even eaten yet. . . .

The thought brought me up short, it was so stereotypical. Maybe I did have maternal instincts.

"Want to call your mom to come get you?"

"My dad. He won't be home yet."

"Does he have a machine? We could leave a message."

"My dad says machines are for yuppies with nothing better to spend their money on."

"Okay, honey. We'll wait a few minutes then. Have you had breakfast?"

She nodded, barely interested, finally getting up the nerve to say what was on her mind: "Can I watch TV?"

"Sure." She scampered off almost happily. Why hadn't I thought of it? The world's greatest baby-sitter and I wasn't even taking advantage.

It was forty-five minutes before her dad had made the round trip, and as miserable a three-quarters of an hour as I've ever spent. First I went to look for Keil, and despite my frantic wails of *Kiiiiiull!* which must have pierced the neighbors' eardrums, he didn't turn up. Then I went up to try to talk to Libby and was rudely told to get out of there. Thank God Esperanza had opted out of the equation.

I thought maybe I could drink my coffee in peace. It was cold, of course. So I made some more, but found I couldn't sit still and relax. In fact, I didn't need the coffee. I was on full-tilt adrenaline.

I phoned my law partner. "Chris, I'm in a bind."

"You poor peach—you're supposed to be resting."

"Well, something's come up. I need a judge in Monterey."

Quickly I sketched in the details. I could almost see Chris as I talked, stroking her long, gorgeous nose with a long, elegant finger, her face a symphony of sympathy—the project was close to futile, and she knew it as well as I did. Judges hardly ever overrule each other.

As she well knew, judges don't list themselves in the phone book. And not only that, with a problem like I had, I'd do well not just to pick one at random, but to arrive with an introduction. Chris said she'd phone around to find out if we knew anybody who knew anybody. But her tone said she thought Marty'd better say good-bye to her weekend plans.

The back door slammed. "Keil? Are you all right, baby?"

"I'm not a baby." He spoke not at all defiantly, simply stating a fact.

"I'm sorry. Can I make you some breakfast?"

"That's okay. I'll do it." He started rummaging about the kitchen.

Again, the doorbell rang. And the telephone at the same time. Keil answered the phone and began speaking in low tones, making it unnecessary to ask for whom the other bell tolled.

The man on the front steps was in a truly rotten mood. "I've been honking for the last five minutes."

"We were in the back of the house." I stared at him, unnerved, feeling like a kid who'd been reprimanded. "Uh—Esperanza's watching TV. None of us heard you."

"TV! She's not supposed to watch TV!"

Without a trace of a warning, tears arrived in my eyes and overflowed. I was crying like a kid in front of a perfect stranger—and the perfect part, from what I could see, was an apt description of his physique, at any rate.

"I didn't know that," I said, like the five-year-old I felt. "How could I know that?"

"I'm sorry. I'm really sorry. It's okay. She does it all the time, anyway. It's no big deal. Really."

Wiping tears with my bare hand, I said, "Come in. I'll get Esperanza," and left before I could further humiliate myself.

When I returned, the stranger had composed himself enough to be civil. He said, "I'm Julio Soto."

"Rebecca Schwartz. Sorry it didn't work out with the kids."

"Is Marty home? I need to ask her something."

"I'm afraid not. Shall I have her call you?"

"No, it's okay. I'll call her later today."

"No, you won't." It was Libby. The three of us turned to find her sitting at the top of the stairs, now dressed in shorts, no trace of tears on her face. "My mom's in jail. She got framed for killing Sadie." She turned and ran.

Julio's tanned face registered shock. "Sadie!"

Esperanza crumpled—sat on the floor, face contorted, knees drawn up, unable to speak. It was like a sitting version of the fetal position. I dropped to my knees. "Honey, are you all right?"

She swiveled her head, panicky, not wanting to deal with someone she didn't know. Julio scooped her up. She whispered, "Daddy, what did she mean?"

"I don't know." He looked at me, seeking confirmation.

I nodded. "Sadie Swedlow was killed last night."

Julio hugged Esperanza to him as if she were a large teddy bear. Bewilderment and trouble spread over his face, making him look about her age. I'm a sucker for vulnerable men and have more than once gotten in trouble trying to take care of them. I tried to disconnect emotionally. Esperanza sobbed softly into Julio's chest.

Julio said, "I saw a lot of hoopla in front of the aquarium."

"Yes. The police sealed it off. You knew Sadie?"

"She was my boss."

"And Esperanza?"

"They were close. Kids like Sadie. I mean, they liked her. I can't believe she's dead."

"She isn't, Daddy! Sadie can't be dead!" Esperanza wailed it out. She formed fists and started to beat on his chest.

"We'd better go," he said, but over Esperanza's shoulder, he mouthed, "What happened?"

Silently I formed the word, "Murdered."

He blinked, shocked, but nodded to show he understood. "Can I call you about this?"

I nodded. That would be fine. I wasn't interested in married men, and therefore, there wouldn't be a problem.

As he headed out the door, he said, "Are you a neighbor?"

"I'm from San Francisco. I'm Marty's lawyer." At the mention of the word "lawyer," he pursed his lips. He probably knew, along with most of Monterey, the details of Marty's busted marriage.

I couldn't tell what his reaction was to Sadie's death, busy as he was attending to his daughter. But I thought it odd Esperanza should have been so upset. It was normal that the Whitehead kids had been—Sadie was their stepmother, in a de facto sense—but why this kid?

I was exhausted. I needed to do Marty's errand for her, but I didn't dare leave Libby in the state she was in, and anyway, I needed to make sure she ate something. By this time the downstairs was filling up with the smell of grilled cheese sandwiches, which was apparently Keil's idea of breakfast. Libby wasn't the only one who needed to eat—it was getting close to noon, and Auntie was working up an appetite. I went into the kitchen.

Keil was standing over the stove wolfing down a grilled cheese. The table was neatly set for one, and he was just pulling another sandwich from the skillet. He delivered it by spatula to the plate on the table. "That's for you."

"Me? You made a sandwich for me?"

"Yeah."

I couldn't get over it. Here was a twelve-year-old whose mother was in jail, whose stepmother was dead, whose dad was God knows where, and he was taking care of *me*. To avoid falling at his feet in gratitude, I fell on the sandwich instead.

Keil hollered, "Lib! You want a grilled cheese?" nearly pulverizing my tympana. I put my hands over my ears.

Keil looked ashamed, caught being a kid. "Sorry."

Deep silence reigned from upstairs. I knew I should go up. I really should try again. But I couldn't find the reserve strength right then.

Keil seemed to be reading my thoughts. "She puts everybody through changes."

The doorbell rang, the front door opened, and someone with heavy footsteps trooped through the house. I hoped it was someone friendly.

"Grandma."

"Hello, Keil. Come kiss your old grandma."

Reluctantly Keil stepped forward and would have given her a kiss on the cheek, but she engulfed him. She wasn't particularly fat and she wasn't praticularly grandmotherly, but it was already obvious she was a strong presence.

She turned to me. "Ava Langford. You must be the lawyer."

I took the hand she offered. "Rebecca Schwartz."

"How's Marty?" The question was sympathetic, but the

brown eyes were full of judgment; of whom, I didn't know yet.

"Doing very well," I said. "Staying calm."

"Cool as a cucumber. Libby?"

"Upstairs. She's very upset."

"She's just trying to get attention. That's the way she is. Keil! This place smells like a fast-food joint." She opened two windows over the sink as she asked, "Will you be staying?"

She wasn't tall, this woman, about five five or six, I'd say, and she was built strong. She was deep-bosomed and heavy-bellied, and she didn't have much of a waist. Her hair was a rich brown—not a gray hair in sight—and it was a little wavy. She would have been a handsome woman if it hadn't been for her eyes. They made me nervous.

I made a quick decision. "Yes. Until I get Marty out of jail."

I didn't want to stay. I wanted like hell to move to a quiet B&B, but something was holding me here—Libby. I had no idea why. She scared me. I didn't know how to talk to her or how to help her. Keil could probably take care of half a dozen kids like her without even breaking into a sweat. She didn't need me and there probably wasn't a damn thing I could do for her. I just thought I ought to stay, that was all.

"I have to do an errand for Marty. I'd better go get dressed."

Ava followed me upstairs. "Is there food in the house for the weekend? If I know Marty, there's not. I'd better go shopping and get things under control."

I went into my room and heard her go into Libby's. "Libby? It's Grandma! Aren't you glad to see Grandma?"

"No!"

"Libby! I'm ashamed of you. Your mama's in jail and you're acting like a two-year-old. How's that going to help

DEAD IN THE WATER

your mom? After all she's been through, I'd think you could act a little more grown-up."

"I'm playing with my Barbies now."

"Grandma came all the way from Walnut Creek and you won't even give her a hug."

The shower into which I gratefully stepped drowned them out.

As I was putting on my makeup, someone knocked softly at my door. "Come in."

Libby did, and made herself at home, sitting on my bed and bouncing. "Can you get Mommy out of jail?"

"Yes, honey. Absolutely. It might not be today, but she'll be home by Monday at the latest. I promise."

"What happened to Sadie? I forgot to ask."

"Well, I think she really did get murdered. Somebody stabbed her."

She found a loose thread in the bedspread to play with. "Mommy didn't do it, did she? It really is a mistake, right?"

"Of course it is."

Anyway, I didn't *think* her mommy did it. I certainly hoped not.

She had an alibi, didn't she?

I wasn't being set up, was I?

CHAPTER 5

Cannery Row was pandemonium. It was a Saturday, the biggest day for aquarium visitors. People were arriving in flocks, but the place was still roped off with yellow crime scene tape. Some left quietly, others stayed to rubberneck. Some, who had driven a hundred miles or more, wanted to argue.

Nice-looking young uninformed police were keeping the mob at bay. A couple, looking exhausted, hovered on the sidelines, apparently taking a break. One of them accosted me. "Hey, aren't you Whitehead's lawyer?"

"Yes." I stared. I'd never seen the man before in my life. What could he want?

"Did you hear scientists are replacing white rats with defense attorneys?"

"Heard about that," I said. "How many cops does it take to change a light bulb?"

For about six months everybody in the world was plaguing lawyers with the rat gag. "There are more defense lawyers," the wag would intone. "The lab assistants don't get as attached to them. And there's nothing they won't do."

It reminded me of the joke about men and sex that made the rounds about the same time: "Why do men reach orgasm faster than women?"

The teller was always male. The answer was "Who cares?" The women in the crowd never found it funny.

Sometimes it's tough being both female and a lawyer. One has trials, they both have tribulations.

Before the young cop could take the bait about the light bulb (I hadn't an answer for him), I headed back to the rear of the building.

There were two rear entrances—the gate through which Marty and I had come the night before, and a nearer one, close to the building, that you could reach from a hiking and biking trail. The crowd had discovered that one. I kept walking back to the parking lot gate, and saw that it was deserted except for its uniformed guard.

I crossed to the Tin Cannery Building, found a phone booth, called the aquarium, and spoke to a female operator. Everyone wanted to be in the thick of things, so I let her talk to someone important.

"This is Special Agent Stone from the FBI. I need to speak with whoever's in charge there."

"I'll put you through to Mr. Nowell."

She rang through and a brusque male voice said, "Warren Nowell."

"Mr. Nowell, this is Rebecca Schwartz. I'm Marty Whitehead's attorney and she asked me to pick something up for her—"

"I heard a rumor Marty's been arrested. Surely that can't be right."

"Let's say she's being held at the police station."

He drew in his breath. "After all she's been through!"

"Thanks. I appreciate the sympathy, and I'll convey it to Marty. But listen, back to my errand. Do you think—"

"I'd love to, but I don't see how I can do a thing for you. The police said not to let anyone in except employees who have to get in to work."

"I see. You've got quite a mess on your hands, haven't you?"

"It's pretty rough. How's Marty doing, anyway?"

"Fine, under the circumstances. She particularly asked me to talk to you—she seemed to think you'd be the person in charge."

"Gee, I really wish I could help, but there's a cop at every entrance. Tell you what—maybe I could have someone bring down whatever it is."

"Unfortunately she wasn't quite sure where it is. She asked me to look for it."

He laughed, a little smugly, I thought. "Well, if you can charm some policeman, you're certainly welcome to do that."

How hard could that be, now that I knew what it took to get in? I was glad I was dressed in jeans and running shoes, and I was glad the young cop at the back gate looked more bored than alert. I tensed my body to give me stage presence, the way I did for court appearances.

"Hi," I said. "Awful about Sadie, isn't it?"

The young cop put on his grim look, the one students are required to learn on the first day of school at police academies across the nation. "Pretty bad."

"I'm Rebecca Schwartz. I work with the sea otters?" I made the sentence a question so I'd sound properly submissive—almost as little and cute as one of the fuzzy beasts I'd mentioned.

"You do? My kid loves those things. He can watch them for hours."

"I know you. You belong to Friends of the Sea Otter."

He looked wary. "No, I—"

"Would you like to join? I think I've got a brochure here." I rummaged in my purse. "We really need your support— there's only three thousand California sea otters left in the wild, and one good oil spill could wipe every one of them out. Did you know that?

"Miss—uh—Schmidt—"

"Schwartz." I gave him a great big, all-American, conservationist grin. "You know, they're not like birds. Our feathered friends—'pelagic birds,' we biologists call them—do pretty well unless they get oil all over them. With an otter it's like Brylcreem—a little dab'll do him." I cut my throat with my finger. "And it's not true they're eating all the shell-fish. An abalone's just a giant snail in the first place, did you know that? I bet you wouldn't eat little escargots, so why would you eat a giant escargot? And anyway, think about it. Three thousand sea otters and millions of human beings—who do you really think is gobbling up the goodies?"

He stepped away from me. I was charming him like a mongoose charms a cobra.

He was still groping for a polite squelch when I stepped back myself. "I'm so sorry. I was being pushy."

A warm blanket of relief spread over him. "It's okay. Are abalones really snails?"

"Honest."

"Yick. Wait'll I tell my brother-in-law. He hates snails. Loves abalone. This'll kill him."

I squinched up my nose, schoolteacher-style. "I'll bet he's a diver, too. Hates sea otters, right?"

He blushed, all but shifted from one foot to the other.

"You, too, I'll bet."

"Hey, I'm a conservationist. I brake for trees."

Having established myself as Miss-Grundy-of-the-deep-blue-sea, I permitted myself to point a finger in his face.

"O-ho. You're a funny one."

We guffawed together like the fun-lovin' fellas he and his brother-in-law were, and then he said, "Okay, Miss Schwartz. Let me see your name tag and I'll let you in."

Name tag! Damn Marty Whitehead's liver and lungs! She could have lent me her damn name tag, and she hadn't even mentioned it.

I said, "Omigod, I don't know if I brought it. See, I switched purses—" As I spoke, I began to pull things out of my purse: a flashlight, a paperback copy of an aquarium book I'd found at Marty's, my calendar. "Oh, no! I really have to feed the little critters. Did you know they have to eat ten times their body weight every six hours?"

My acting teacher had said you could get the effect you wanted just by wanting to. As I kept my eyes lowered and chattered, frantically pulling things from my purse, I imagined a tank full of poor orphaned sea otters, separated from their mothers in stormy seas, and now at the mercy of human beings who were after all only human and sometimes left their name tags at home and therefore couldn't get in to feed them. I imagined how lost and miserable and, above all, *hungry* an otter in such a tank would feel. When I felt genuine tears, I looked up.

"I overslept," I said. "I was supposed to feed them at eight."

Quickly, as if embarrassed at having been caught crying, I looked down again and found my keys, including the ones Marty had turned over to me. "Look, how about if I show you I really do have a key that'll open that gate—wouldn't that prove I work here?"

He looked around to see if he was being observed and I knew I had won.

"Sure," he said. "Hardly anyone remembered their name tag this morning. You guys must have pretty casual security."

I only wished my acting class, before which I was as likely to flub my lines as not, could have seen my award-quality improvisation.

In Marin County, where I grew up, all kids take nearly every kind of lessons they can fit into their schedules—except acting. That could lead to a career in the arts and a life of poverty.

I took acting after I got beat in court by a DA who'd done it—Raymond Fanelli, damn his soul. His *opening* statement

had the jury in tears. By the time the trial was over, they
wanted my client's blood. Since she was a battered wife who'd
finally fought back (if a little too hard), I had plenty of his-
trionic material myself. I'm convinced she'd be a free woman
today if I'd put in a better performance.

Anyway, I did well that day in the parking lot. I later
looked up the actual figures on sea otters, and I wasn't that
far off. But to set the record straight, things are even worse
than I thought—there are actually only seventeen hundred of
them left in California, and opinions vary as to whether one
oil spill would lubricate their way to oblivion. They eat only
a quarter of their body weight daily, which may sound pitiful
compared to the fanciful figure of my imagination, but for
one of us, it would be about forty hamburgers.

An abalone really is a snail.

Once inside, I followed Marty's directions to the third
floor, where, I had learned, most aquarium employees had
their offices.

What Marty hadn't told me was that the place still looked
like a sardine warehouse. No walls had been added, only
those partitions that give you "modular" offices, or, in truth,
no offices at all, but something more like library carrels.
Hers was the fourth or fifth "office" on the right, she'd said—
she couldn't remember exactly, but I was to look for pictures
of Libby and Keil.

The way her directions went, you entered at the left, so
you must cross to the row of cubicles at the far right, I
thought. I was standing at the front of the huge room, trying
to get my bearings, when a fast-moving figure cannoned
down the left row, and passed me.

The runner wore a baseball cap, jeans, and tennies, so that
I hadn't heard him until it was almost too late, and he had
his head down, so I couldn't see his face. From the back, I
got a glimpse of a blue T-shirt that said Monterey Bay Aquar-

ium between the shoulder blades. It was a slight figure, like a small man, but I couldn't have sworn it wasn't a woman or even a kid. I stepped out of the way just in time, feeling the breeze, and stood for a minute recovering my equilibrium.

Then, without even considering the consequences, I wheeled and followed, back through the office door and down the stairs to a choice of three more doors. Fortunately, one was just snicking shut. I tried it, but I needed Marty's key to open it. It took a couple of lifetimes, but still, when I was in, I could hear the muted thud of fast-moving Reeboks somewhere in the distance.

I knew where I was, vaguely. I had come out near the aquarists' offices, near the staff library. Marty and I had been here the night before. I retraced our steps through the volunteers' offices, and the volunteer and staff lounge, and out to an area where you could go into one of several small rooms, go downstairs, or go through double doors into the behind-the-scenes feeding area. You would have to unlock a door to go behind the scenes, and once through the area, back in the aquarium proper, you wouldn't be able to blend into the crowd, because the place was empty today. Figuring I might be wasting precious time, I peered into the graphics and publications offices, didn't see places to hide, and hit the stairs.

I didn't hear a thing. Undaunted, I raced down them and tore open the door at the bottom, only to face a crowd of thousands. I was now on Cannery Row, and the cop who'd tried to tell me the white rat joke was on guard at this entrance. "I'll bite," he said. "How many cops *does* it take?"

I stared at him, utterly uncomprehending.

"To change a light bulb," he said.

"Listen, did a guy in a baseball hat just come through here?"

"Uh-uh. I asked first."

"Officer, this is important. Anyway, I forget the punch line."

"Hey, Counselor, you know what? I got some good news for you. It's not working out in those labs. They finally realized the rats were smarter."

Seething, I walked slowly back to the third floor, giving myself plenty of time to cool off. As soon as I opened the door of the huge warehouse of offices, I heard a voice—one I recognized as Warren Nowell's—raised in what could only be a chewing-out.

Gently I let myself in, tiptoed to Marty's cubicle (the fifth one, it turned out), ducked into it, and peeked around the corner. At the front of the room—or the rear if you considered the entrance the front—there was a receptionist's desk and a genuine private office to the right. A man—Nowell, by his voice—was standing in the doorway of the office, more or less yelling.

"What the hell do you think you're doing here? Don't you realize you could be tampering with evidence in a murder case?"

"Oh, Warren, pipe down." It was Julio Soto's voice, emanating from the enclosed office. With the place empty as it was, sounds carried beautifully.

I heard the noise of someone opening drawers and rummaging in them. Remembering my own mission, I looked at the calendar on Marty's desk. It was still turned to Friday, the night before. Damn her, she'd lied to me—she had had a date the night before. Still keeping both ears open, I started flipping through her calendar, to see if there was a pattern of rendezvous, and if so, how far back it went.

I heard Warren say, "Sorry. I'm not mad at you. I'm just— a lot's happened this morning, that's all. I'm sorry I snapped. But I will have to ask you to stop rifling Sadie's desk."

The rummaging noise stopped. I tried opening Marty's top drawer, to look for the note, but it stuck. Thinking it might make an awful noise if I forced it, I put it off for a minute. Frankly, I didn't want to interrupt the conversation a few feet away.

Julio said, rather nastily, I thought, "What gives you that authority?"

"I'm acting director."

"I beg your pardon? How could that be? The board can't have had time to meet."

"Well, then, make it acting acting director. The president phoned this morning and asked if I'd take care of things until they can meet—which they're doing this afternoon—to make it official."

"You sound very sure of yourself."

"He sounded pretty definite. Do you mind if I ask you what you're looking for?"

"Oh—uh—something I lent Sadie. Mmm—well, none of your business, Warren. No hard feelings, I hope? And congratulations."

"Thanks."

There was a pause while I imagined them shaking hands, and then I heard them starting to leave, walking toward me. If I started searching then, they'd almost certainly hear me, and I didn't think Warren, despite what he'd rashly said over the phone, was going to give me a free hand.

My purse wasn't large enough to fit the calendar in. I'd brought a plastic bag for it, but I'd have to get it out and unfold it—there wasn't time. I tore off the "Friday" leaf of the calendar—there had been other dates, so it wasn't the ultimate solution, but it was all I could do for now.

Before I had time to duck out of sight, they were parallel with the cubicle. They stopped—staring straight at me. Julio said, "Rebecca Schwartz, how on earth did you get in?"

"Charmed a policeman," I said.

His companion was around five ten and overweight. He had thin, curly hair and wore glasses. For some unfathomable reason, he held up his jeans with a belt sporting a giant buckle that looked like a rodeo prize. Fat under his T-shirt rippled like Jell-O around the edges of the buckle. There was something a little vague about him.

He said, "You must be a very resourceful person."

"And you must be Warren Nowell. I recognize your voice."

"What did you need to pick up for Marty?"

"Just some papers she wanted."

"I think I have to reconsider what I told you on the phone."

"I was afraid of that." I shrugged and stepped out.

The three of us walked as far as the door, but Warren came no farther, making it clear he was escorting us out, where we belonged. When Julio and I were alone, I asked how Esperanza was.

He looked miserable. "Awful. Near-catatonic, to tell you the truth. I don't know what to do."

I must have looked baffled.

He said, "I'm sort of new at single parenthood."

An odd ringing sounded in my ear as I caught his implication. My heart pounded. But these were not the beginnings of tender feelings. Oh, no. Not when I hadn't even had a chance to mourn Rob yet. Not with Marty cooling her heels in the hoosegow. And certainly not, knowing what I knew. Marty's calendar for Friday night had said "6:30—J."

The pounding was fear. The ringing was a built-in alarm bell.

"You wouldn't have time for coffee, would you?"

"Sure," I said. Alarm bell be damned.

I called Chris from the restaurant.

"Got a name and number for you. Judge Serita Reyes— new on the bench, said to be eminently reasonable. And female. Maybe she has kids and she'll be sympathetic."

"Who knows her?"

"Bruce—uh—Pigball."

"Parton." Chris had a repertoire of made-up words she used when she couldn't think of real ones—and she could almost never remember names. But I had no problem figuring out who she meant; Bruce had been in my class at Boalt.

"He's separated from his wife, by the way—he made a special point of telling me—and asking about you."

"Chris, stop being southern, would you? I can't think about that right now."

"Of course not. He's for later, maybe." She gave me the judge's number.

I dialed eagerly, mentally preparing my spiel, and got not so much as an answering machine. I dialed again. Nothing.

So I called Bruce for her address. No luck there either.

Coming back from the phone, I found I had trouble believing the handsome man in the white pants and light yellow sweatshirt was actually waiting for me. This Julio was something else in the looks department, and the worried frown he wore was the most appealing thing about him. I was truly reverting to form. Rob wasn't the vulnerable type at all, but the minute he was out of my sight, I was up to my old tricks. I pulled in my energy and tried to think of this as an exercise in information gathering.

Julio looked oddly sad when he smiled. "They have cappuccino here."

"Good. I'd love some." Maybe it would sharpen my rapidly dulling faculties. "Could I ask you a question?"

"Sure."

"What were you looking for in Sadie's office?"

"Oh, that. Something of Esperanza's—a rock or something she found on the beach."

"Why did Sadie have it?"

He opened his arms in the universal helpless gesture. "They were playing some sort of game—I don't know. They were close."

"Esperanza and Sadie?"

Remembering what Marty had said, I wondered if Sadie had once been Esperanza's stand-in stepmother. But Julio said, "When Don started living with her, Libby naturally started spending a lot of time with the two of them. Esperanza went over to spend a weekend and fell in love. It was that simple. Sometimes she'd come over to the aquarium after school, and do you think she'd ask to see me? Not first, anyway. That's why Sadie's death hit her so hard."

I sipped my cappuccino.

"I don't know," said Julio. "I guess she misses her mother."

"Is this the first time she's been away from her?"

"For this long, yes. I've had her all summer."

"That must have been nice."

"Uh-huh. And hard. Really hard. I'd have been lost without Libby and Amber, another kid whose dad works with Marty and me."

"Do you miss her mom, too?"

He thought it over. "I don't guess I do anymore. She went back to Santa Barbara—we're both from there. Out of sight, out of mind, I guess."

I must have winced, because he said, "I didn't mean that the way you think. I meant that it seems more final when you don't see the person every day."

"Santa Barbara's nice."

He smiled wryly. "A nice place to be from. All Hispanics are called Mexicans there."

"Even second-generation ones?"

"Even Salvadorans." His mouth twitched briefly as if he meant to smile when he said it, but couldn't quite manage. "I wish Esperanza could grow up in a friendlier atmosphere. But Sylvia thinks she's better off being near her grandparents. I don't know, maybe she's right. At least she'll never have to do domestic service like they did."

"What's her mom do?"

"Social worker. That's why she went back. Many good works crying out to be done."

"But you prefer fish."

"Any day." His teeth were almost translucent. His lips were so full, they looked slightly puckered even in repose. When he smiled, I couldn't take my eyes off his mouth.

"What exactly do you do at the aquarium?"

"Marine biologist. We all are, those of us in husbandry. We don't all collect, though; that's the best part."

"Of course. That's where the adventure is." We both smiled, and we locked eyes. I looked away quickly. Visual caresses weren't what I was there for.

"I want to start teaching Esperanza to snorkel, but she doesn't seem all that interested."

"She's got a hell of a lot on her mind right now, with her parents breaking up—"

"Do you have kids?"

"No, why?"

"I was hoping you could help me with mine."

"That's an odd request—don't you have a woman friend you could ask?"

He shrugged. "That's my problem. Marty's in jail and Sadie's dead." His voice dropped on the last two words, and I thought it was more than some societal acknowledgment of her death.

"Did you like her? Sadie?"

"Very much." The words were so heartfelt, I didn't dare press him further on the subject. "And Esperanza loved her. Rebecca—" His eyes were pleading and hurt. "I know this sounds strange, but could you come home with me and talk to her?"

I was at a loss. "Talk to her? What would I say?"

"I don't know. She liked you. She told me so."

If this was a sexual ploy, it was the oddest one I'd ever encountered. But if it wasn't that, what was it?

"I think maybe I should take her to a doctor. Maybe she's in shock or something."

"Why do you say that?"

"She won't speak, except to mention the rock or whatever it is. She won't even give it a name. She calls it 'the white thing.' She's acting as if Sadie's death had something to do with it."

My ears perked up. "You mean, as if someone killed her for it?"

Ho looked confused and frustrated. "I don't know. She's not making sense. Something's going on. She's acting as if she's afraid of me."

CHAPTER 6

I couldn't believe what I saw in Julio's living room—a huge saltwater aquarium. And other than that, precious little, as if Sylvia had taken the furniture and he'd replaced it with odds and ends.

"You like the aquarium?"

"Was I staring?"

"It's kind of predictable, I guess."

"It's not that; it's just that—" I stopped. I was damned if I was going to tell him we had this huge thing in common, as if this were a date or something. "It's very nice."

It was quite different from mine, much bigger for one thing, three hundred gallons maybe. And mine was heated, so I could keep tropical fish; his was a cold one. He kept the same sorts of fishes in it that they did in the big aquarium—the ones found in Monterey Bay.

"I keep mostly juvenile things in it—little blue rockfish, chili peppers, mysid shrimps, perch, gunnels—"

"There's a grunt sculpin!" I didn't mean to show off, but I love those funny little fellows.

"You seem to know your fish."

"Oh, look—a baby wolf eel." I could just see its head in a little rock cave Julio had built for it.

He grinned. "Cecil the sea serpent. Esperanza hates him. She doesn't care much for snaky fish."

"Omigod! What is *that*?"

"What?"

"That thing that looks like a—a—"

He stared at my pointing finger. "A dog turd?"

"To put it delicately."

"That's how Esperanza puts it. And talk about something she hates! Wow, does she hate them—with a deep, primal loathing the way some people hate spiders. Libby, too—all the kids do. Can't say that I blame them either. Some things are hard even for an aquarist to stomach. It's a hagfish—I've got three of them in there. Disgusting, but they'll keep your tank clean for you."

"A hagfish?"

"Otherwise knows as a slime eel. Does that ring a bell?"

I shook my head. "I guess I've led a more sheltered life than I thought."

"No eyes; one rasping tooth." He shuddered. "Among its other charming qualities, it can tie itself in knots."

"What about the slime?"

But Esperanza, who had heretofore not uttered a peep, called, "Daddy, are you back? Did you get it?"

"Uh-oh." Julio looked sheepish, a provider who'd failed to bring home the bacon. "I guess I'd better break the news."

"I didn't realize she was here. She was so quiet."

He sighed. "That's how she's been."

"I mean, I guess I imagined you'd left her with a neighbor."

He saw what I was getting at. "You don't think I should have left her alone?"

"She seems so little."

"She's just short, like her mom. She's ten—you don't think that's old enough?"

I considered. "I guess so."

It was comical, really. I could tell he genuinely didn't know if she was old enough to be left alone, and he thought I might because I'm a woman. I hadn't a clue. Who did know anything about kids, and how did they find out? I'd never thought to wonder before.

"I'll tell her the bad news. Then you can go in." Julio walked to the back of the house, and I thought I could hear a drone, his voice. There was one stifled wail and nothing else from Esperanza.

He came back looking like some sitcom depiction of an expectant father in a waiting room—terrified by the alien world of women and children. "She's a wreck."

"Shall I go in alone, or do you want to come?"

But he was staring past me, out the window. "Here comes Ricky. Maybe Amber's with him."

I remembered that Amber was a young friend of Esperanza's, and seeing a boy—or young man—getting out of his car, I thought he might be her brother. He was wearing a baseball cap, jeans, and tennies. He was fairly slight and fairly short—maybe a boy and maybe a man. Almost certainly the fleeing figure I'd so impulsively chased.

Clearly hoping for a juvenile distraction, Julio strode past me and opened the door. "Ricky, boy, come in. Did you bring Amber?'

"Amber's grounded. We're talking about a very, very naughty girl."

"What'd she do?"

"Something so bad, I don't even want to say." He came in, spotted me, and went, without missing a beat, into a none-too-subtle once-over. He wasn't Amber's brother. Either he was another single father or married life didn't suit him.

"Ricky Flynn, Rebecca Schwartz," said Julio.

I nodded, not offering to shake. Ricky's staring had put me off.

Ricky nodded back, gave me a worried look—did he recognize me?—and turned to Julio, all but jerking his head in my direction, spelling out that he wished I weren't there. A polite person would have left the room. I thought I'd learn more if I stayed.

Ricky said, "Hey, man, I've got to talk to you."

"Ricky, it's not a good time. Esperanza's really flattened by Sadie's death."

"Oh, God! It's true." Ricky looked as if he might cry. "That's what I came by to ask. I thought it was just some crazy rumor. Marty—"

Julio looked a warning. "Rebecca's Marty's lawyer," he said quickly.

"You're Marty's lawyer?"

I nodded, slightly amused that he wanted it repeated. On second look, there was something appealing about Ricky, and it was the thing that had put me off at first—the boyish quality that included staring like a teenager. He took off the baseball hat and ran a hand through light hair that was cut stylishly spiky, but wouldn't stand up right after its mashing. Some of it sagged and some stuck up in tufts, affording an amusingly zany look that went well with his freckles. I thought he was younger than Julio, but I couldn't be sure. It was hard to imagine him a father.

He blurted, "I heard Marty murdered her."

"You did? Maybe you better tell me about it."

He flushed. "I thought it was just a rumor." He stuffed his hands in his jeans and stared at his tennis shoes. "It's really true, huh?"

"It's really true someone murdered her. Where were *you* last night between six and eight?"

"Me?" He seemed deeply shocked by the question. "Having dinner with Amber."

"Just kidding."

"Oh." To Julio he said, "This really messes me up, man."

"Ricky, could we talk about it later?"

"Oh, yeah. Sorry—see you later." He gave me a nervous,

surreptitious grin and more or less stumbled out, tripping
over his toes. The look reminded me of a little kid who
covers his face and thinks he's invisible. Ricky might be a
puer eternus, but it's the sort of thing lots of grown-ups do.

The funny thing is that it usually works, I've noticed. When
one person telegraphs he wants to keep something secret,
others usually enter into a silent conspiracy to help him do
it, even when it's much to their disadvantage. And so my
natural impulse was to respect Ricky's privacy. I ignored it.

"I think I made him uncomfortable," I said. "He gave
me a funny look when he left."

"You didn't make him uncomfortable. He thought you
were swell."

"It seemed as if he really had something on his mind."

"Ricky overdramatizes."

Oh, well. Discretion is a good quality in a man.

All this time, there hadn't been a peep out of Esperanza.
We found her lying on her bed staring at the wall.

Julio said, "*Nena*, I've brought Rebecca. You know—the
nice lady from Libby's? I thought you might want to talk to
her."

No answer.

The hopelessness of the whole idea swept over me like a
bucket of cold water. And I was furious. Esperanza had been
afraid of me before, she'd be afraid of me now. I was a
stranger. She wasn't going to talk to me.

Now I saw exactly why Julio had brought me here. This
was no sexual ploy, it was a sexist one. Dealing with difficult children was women's work and he'd simply never
learned how to do it. He'd told me the truth—I was sure
he did feel helpless in the face of Esperanza's withdrawal.
Instead of having the balls to break through, figure it out,
do what had to be done, he'd recruited me. But I wasn't

really angry at him. I was pissed off because I felt as much at a loss as he did.

Julio stayed at the threshold while I crept in and sat on the bed, not sure whether the closeness would be comforting or threatening. I started winging it, babbling, more or less stream-of-consciousness-style, hoping I'd hit on something that got a response.

"You know, Libby loved Sadie very much, too. It's going to be very hard for both of you without her, and I understand how bad you feel. I want you to know that it's okay to cry and feel as bad as you need to feel and that that feeling will go away, maybe not today, maybe not tomorrow—"

I stopped to get hold of myself, hoping she was too young to have seen *Casablanca*. I got up the nerve to stroke her hair, and to my surprise, she turned on her back and looked at me. Her eyes flicked to Julio, and I thought I saw fear in them—he had said she seemed afraid of him—and instinctively I turned, perhaps to see if I could see what she saw. But Julio smiled a quiet smile and left.

The coward, I thought, but my heart wasn't in it. I knew he had done the right thing, leaving us alone.

What next? It was anybody's guess what was troubling her—other than simple grief—but that flicker of fear made me think there *was* something. Why would a child be afraid of her father?

The first thing that came up made my throat go dry. I smashed it down quickly and tried to think. But my mind wouldn't leave it. I remembered everything I'd ever heard about molested children—that is, about our reactions to them. We try to pretend it didn't happen. We don't want to believe it and we don't listen. I couldn't fall into that trap. I had to face it.

"Sweetheart, is there something you need to talk to me about?"

Terror. Absolute, unadulterated terror spread like a blush

on her small face. She shook her head violently. I pretended
not to notice. I smiled, or maybe grimaced; anyway, I went
through the motion. "Good. Because if anybody hurt you, I
wouldn't let them get away with it. Adults are supposed to
protect kids, and I'd do that. I'd make sure they never hurt
you again."

I saw the relief even before I started the protection prom-
ises. Did she believe me? Was I winning her confidence?

"Has someone hurt you?"

She shook her head, eyes bland, telling me I was completely off base.

"Are things okay between you and your dad?"

Fear flickered again. Having faced the incest specter (and
gotten nowhere), I tried to see beyond it. Why else might a
child be afraid of her father?

Because she had a guilty secret. *Or thought she had.*

That must be it. Aha, I had it now for sure.

"You know, Esperanza," I intoned importantly, "what
happened to Sadie was really awful, but you couldn't stop it
from happening. A lot of times people feel guilty when
someone dies, but it's only a feeling, it's not real. I mean,
they feel that way even though they couldn't possibly have
had anything to do with the person's death."

Tears started in the brown eyes, and a sob from the
deep wracked her body upright and into my arms. She
clung to me like a barnacle to a gray whale, her body
heaving as if she were retching, and I knew that it felt
that way to her. I was swept to my own childhood crying
jags, to the overwhelming feeling of needing to be rid of
something.

Unexpectedly she spoke to me. "Did they really put Marty
in jail?"

"I'm afraid they did, but she won't have to stay there long.
They're going to let her out pretty soon."

She pulled away from me, but maintained eye contact,

kept sitting. She seemed to be coming out of her waking coma.

"Is jail worse than hell?"

"To tell you the truth, not everyone believes in hell."

"They don't? It isn't a real place?"

"Some people think it is. But no one's ever been there and come back, so no one knows for sure."

"Jail's real, though, huh?"

"Yes, but you know what? I'm a lawyer—did you know that?"

"You are?"

"Uh-huh. And that makes me an officer of the court. The law says you can only go to jail if you're guilty. As an officer of the court, I pronounce you Not Guilty."

She lay back on her pillow, her face infinitely sad. I had said the wrong thing.

Desperate to keep her from retreating again, I said, "Can we be friends, you and I?"

She nodded once, vaguely, her heart not in it, just pleasing a grown-up.

"I'll help you no matter what, Esperanza. And I can do that because I'm a lawyer. Do you believe that?" (I'd heard that kids know instinctively when you're feeding them bilge water, but I was gambling that it wasn't true.)

She nodded again. This time did I see a faint glimmer of hope? Probably not, but I bulled forward.

"You lost a good friend when you lost Sadie, and I think you need another one. I'd like it to be me." I had a sudden twinge. Was I being manipulative? Quickly I said, "I don't mean you have to do anything for me or even talk to me if you don't want to. But I want you to know you can if you like."

I waited a moment. "Would you like to tell me about the white thing?"

She turned to the wall.

"I just thought that, since you trusted Sadie with it, and I'm your friend now, that you might trust me."

Dead silence.

"Okay, I understand. I was just wondering—a thing like that—what did it look like, exactly?"

Her voice was flat, a monotone, as if she were on drugs. "Like a brain."

Julio came in. "You two doing okay?"

I patted a small leg. "You know, you've got a terrific little girl here."

"Don't I know it."

A tiny sniff escaped the huddled-up heap on the bed—a stifled sob, I thought. Julio said, "You know what Esperanza really loves?"

"Pizza?"

"Besides that."

"Spaghetti?"

"Besides that, too."

"Movies."

"As long as nothing awful happens to any fuzzy animal. But something else."

"Sea otters!"

"Bingo! Bingo! The grand prize for Rebecca! But what I meant was, the way she really likes to look at the sea otters is from a boat. Isn't that right, *Nena*?" He paused for an answer, received none, and continued undaunted in the same vein. "So guess what we're going to do this afternoon? We're going for a sail! That is, if Esperanza wants to—"

He winked at me, so confident was he this was an offer she couldn't refuse.

And she didn't refuse. She simply kept her own silent, ominous counsel.

"Want to go with us, Rebecca?"

"I don't know. Libby and Keil—"

"We'll all go! It's more fun that way—isn't it, *Nena*?"

Esperanza seemed interested. She didn't face us, but she broke her gravelike silence: "Can Amber go, too?"

"Amber's grounded. Ricky came by and said—"

She sat up, her golden face white. "What? What did she do?"

"He wouldn't tell us. He just said it was so bad he didn't want to talk about it."

She rolled off the bed, running, but she stopped suddenly, stood a moment, and then started to fall.

Julio moved quickly, catching her as she sank to her knees. "Head down, *Nena*. Head down." To me he said, "It's all right. It's all right. She's just fainted. It's not a seizure or anything. She's okay!" He was shouting.

I saw that her face was sweaty now. Julio fanned her with an opened book, and elevated her feet. In a moment she woke up, and the look in her eyes said she didn't need to go to hell to know what it was like. "You fainted again, baby."

She closed her eyes again, to get away, I thought. When we had put cold washcloths on her face and given her juice, we left. It seemed to be what she wanted.

Julio stared at his aquarium, and it gave me such a start, I said, "I do that. I stare at mine when I'm upset."

"You have an aquarium?"

"Saltwater tropical. Smaller than yours—only a hundred gallons."

"Well." He seemed to want to smile, but couldn't bring himself to do it right then.

"That's what Marty and I have in common."

He patted his pockets, caught himself, and looked at me sheepishly. "I haven't done that in ten years. Haven't smoked in twelve."

"I'd better go."

He ignored me. "She fainted once before—when Sylvia and I told her we were getting divorced."

A small voice interrupted. "Dad?"

Julio and I smiled conspiratorially, two kids who'd gotten a wish.

"Yes, honey?"

"What time are we going sailing?"

CHAPTER 7

If it had to be a sunset cruise, I was going to do one little thing first. Maybe not get Marty out of jail, but at least give her a piece of my mind. And there was one other thing I wanted to check on.

Jacobson, apparently working all weekend, was in her office, which looked out on a little lemon grove. It was a cheerful place for such business to be conducted, very different from San Francisco's Hall of Justice, which is gray (except for the rose marble on the first floor), urban, and all business.

"Hello, Paula. I was just wondering—has the autopsy been done yet?"

"I'm sorry, but I really can't give out that information."

"Sure you can. I bet it has been done—or it's scheduled for sometime today, right? I mean, how many homicides do you have around here?"

"Two in a year would be a record," she said dryly.

"Who's the DA assigned to the case?"

"Todd Greenberg. Why?"

"What did he think of your case?"

"Why don't you ask him?"

"I will. But as long as I'm here, why don't you let me see the autopsy report?"

"Sorry." She gave me a pitying look and went back to her paperwork.

I kind of liked what I heard. She was a little more defensive than she'd had to be. I wondered if Greenberg wasn't as thrilled with her airtight case as she and Tillman were.

Perhaps fifteen feet away from the pleasant office with the view of a lemon grove, just around the corner, was as nasty a jail as—well, frankly, as jail always is. This one was painted a deep turquoise instead of black or gray, but bars are bars. It seemed ten degrees colder after Tillman turned the over-size key in the lock and led me inside. His feet—mine were in noiseless tennis shoes—echoed in the corridor. Three steps in, I was deeply depressed, and Marty's cellblock was at the other end of the place.

She was standing, waiting for me, in the business suit I'd left her in, the same one she'd worn to work the day before.

Her cell nearly made me cry, and would have, I suspect, if I'd been younger and less experienced and not so angry with her. That horrible chestnut "She's made her bed—" popped up, but it was hard to be too punitive when the bed in question was a concrete bunk built into the wall. It had on it only a mattress, a pillow, and a folded-up blanket.

The only other furniture, if you could call it that, was a no-frills metal toilet.

She spoke first. "What time is it? They took my watch."

"Around two, I think. Have they fed you?"

"Two TV dinners already today, but of course, I didn't eat them. Do you know what the sodium content of those things is?"

"Didn't eat them? You were expecting radicchio with a little warm chèvre?"

We both sat on the bunk.

"It's no big deal. I needed to lose weight anyway. It's inconceivably boring in here, though. I wish I'd taken a meditation class, but there never seemed to be time. Did you know you're not allowed any reading material? Or panty hose—how about that one?" She held out a bare foot, shod in a neat black pump. "You might strangle yourself with them."

"But they let you take a shower, of course."

Of course they hadn't. I was rubbing it in. I was getting madder by the moment, and not only at her—at myself for wasting sympathy on her. "Marty Whitehead, you lied to me."

Her face lit up. "You've been to my office? Did you bring the stuff?"

"No, I did not bring the stuff. I had to impersonate a member of the staff to get in, and then I was caught in the act, so I didn't get anything out of the building—except this." I produced the calendar leaf for the night before. "You couldn't have killed her, damn you! You were somewhere screwing your brains out."

I admit I made this speech partly in case the cell was bugged—a ridiculous idea for a quiet town like Monterey.

"You sound mad that I didn't kill her. Whose side are you on, anyway?"

"I'm mad because only a born victim would spend a night in jail to protect a man, and a born victim is a dead loser in court, and I don't want one for a client."

"Okay, okay. I'll get another lawyer."

"That won't solve your problem. Another lawyer's going to feel exactly the same way—like doing anything in the world besides stand around watching you cut your own throat. Tell me the guy's name, Marty. Tell Jacobson and Tillman and walk away from this. He got himself into this mess, you didn't. Who cares about him? Think of Libby and Keil, dammit!"

Her refusal to think of her kids seemed so heartless, I wanted to bang her head against the bars. Recent encounters with ten-year-olds had left me feeling protective and righteous.

"Rebecca, I don't have an alibi. He stood me up."

"He stood you up. Sure he stood you up. First your date wasn't this Friday, it was last Friday, and now he stood you up. If your own lawyer can't trust you, how's a jury supposed to?"

She said nothing.

"The guy's married, I suppose. Is that it?" Suddenly I thought I knew what she was up to, and I was sorry for the remark about Libby and Keil. "Wait a minute. You're afraid of a custody battle, aren't you?"

She nodded, maybe blinking tears, maybe not, I couldn't tell.

"Well, get it out of your head. If you have to stand trial, even if you're not convicted, those kids are going to have to go through something a whole lot worse than any custody fight in the world. If you're found guilty, it won't be an issue."

I knew I sounded cruel—I'd learned how in acting class. But a good alibi was my best shot at getting her out of this mess. Besides, she was genuinely getting my goat. Self-destructive behavior in a client spells defeat in the courtroom. And I hate defeat.

"I don't expect you to understand."

"Okay. All right. But I'm off this case as soon as you're arraigned."

"I think that'll be best for both of us. Are the kids okay? Did Mother get here?"

"Your mother got here. The kids are not all right. Their mother's in jail, and they're worried."

"Has Don turned up?"

"Not yet."

Ava had called her "cool as a cucumber," and while it wasn't original, I had to admit that mother certainly knew daughter. Her business suit was pretty wilted after thirty hours of constant wear, she was a shadow of herself without her Rolex, and no one could confuse a steel toilet with the seat of power. But Marty was doing business as usual, cool as a whole truckload of cucumbers—cucumbers, in fact, garnishing Pimm's cups being served around a swimming pool. She could have been planning the financial future of the aquarium. "Has an acting director been named?"

"Warren Nowell—at least he said he expected to be."

"Damn! I could have had a shot at it."

"Here we go again. Look, I hate to harp on this, but you're in jail. If you were out of jail—"

"I'm going to be, Rebecca. On Monday at the latest—and frankly, I don't really consider Warren a whole lot of competition. What did you think of him?"

Was she trying to distract me from getting on her case, or was she really this cold? Maybe I'd been wrong about her that night in San Francisco—when I thought she was in denial about the breakup of her marriage. Maybe she just didn't have any feelings.

"He doesn't look like much, but he was acting okay. Using his authority pretty well."

"Oh? I find him unprepossessing. He's well connected, though. You've heard of Katy Montebello?"

I shook my head.

"The former Katy Sheffield. She's probably the aquarium's chief individual benefactor. Companies give more, but I doubt any one person has put up more money than Katy. In fact, she's sponsoring our new exhibit. Anyway, Katy and Warren's mother are best friends. He went to Stanford, but other than that, he's a pretty weak sister."

"What's his job?

"Director of education. Big deal."

"Who's your other biggest competition?"

She tapped her chin. "I don't think Martin would take it—the director of husbandry. Really, unless they went outside—" she shrugged "—it's Warren or me."

"I met someone in husbandry today—Julio Soto."

"Oh, shit! Esperanza was supposed to come over this morning."

"She did. Libby sent her home."

"I forgot all about it. That's really unlike me. I should have had you call Julio—"

"Marty, you're in jail. Give yourself a break."

"This is the way I am. I run like a machine."

I could believe that.

"Tell me, what did you think of Julio?" She smiled almost girlishly.

"He seems very nice."

"No wonder you like fish. You're cold, Rebecca." Her eyes were playful.

"I did happen to notice the mustache and the eyes and the shoulders."

She laughed. "I'll bet you did."

We had slipped back into our old camaraderie. Weird under the circumstances, but I supposed this was Marty's way of coping. For all I knew, it was a front. Maybe as soon as I left, she'd cry into her rough blanket.

I wondered if I was relaxed enough to ask her if Julio was "J." I tried working up to it subtly. "Was he one of Sadie's conquests?"

She laughed. "He's too much man for her. She went in for the Ricky Flynns of the world."

"I met Ricky Flynn, too."

"You really get around, don't you?

"He came over to Julio's—" Too late, I realized I'd said too much.

Marty narrowed her eyes. "Oh. 'Over to Julio's—' "

I lied like a teenager. "I took Esperanza home. Ricky dropped by. Actually, I liked him. I see what Sadie saw in him."

"I'll bet he's worried about losing his job. Warren hates him. With good reason, too. Ricky taunts him."

"About what?"

"About being a stuffed shirt." We both laughed, just two girls in a dorm, having a gabfest.

"So what does Ricky do?"

"He's not even permanently on the staff. Does seasonal work, actually. I mean—not seasonal. Piecework, I guess you'd call it. He's a model-maker."

"A model-maker?"

"Makes models for the exhibits. You want some barnacles the size of your hand, Ricky's your man. A life-sized elephant seal? Actually, he's doing one of those for the new exhibit. He's a genius, but he drinks."

"Drinks?"

"You know, like alcohol? I think that's why Sadie dumped him. Not that he ever was a main squeeze or anything. Ricky's not the type you take to business parties— leave it to Sadie Stoop-Low."

The nickname reminded me that she had said Sadie was unpopular with the staff. It was funny, I hadn't noticed. As I got up to go, Marty called me back. "Rebecca."

"Yes?"

She stared at the floor. "I'm really embarrassed about last night." Mustering all her effort, she met my eyes for the big confession. "About falling apart. I'm not usually like that."

Back at the ranch, Ava had everything out of Marty's kitchen cabinets and on the table. Methodically, she was cleaning each cabinet, a look of utter disgust on her face.

"I'll bet these haven't been cleaned since they moved in. I know they were cleaned then, because I cleaned them."

"Marty and Don are busy people."

"Nothing wrong with those two strong kids they've got."

"I guess clean cabinets are more important to some people than others."

"Marty hates dirt. Last time I was here, I thought I'd

surprise her and scrub the kitchen floor, but Don made me stop in the middle—said it was an 'inappropriate' time to do it.''

''Mmmm.'' I could smell a grievance coming on, and I thought life would be a lot simpler if I could head it off.

She jabbed at a corner with a sponge. ''Three in the afternoon and he had to start cooking dinner!''

I couldn't help it—curiosity got the best of me. ''What was he making?''

''That's not the point—the point is, he and Marty got mad at me for trying to help. And then they had the nerve to ask me to help with dinner. Can you imagine? After that? They were having thirty people over, too.''

''Gosh.'' I began to back out of the room.

''And it was my birthday. They wanted me to work on my own birthday.''

Rebecca, do not say it. Do not say a word about the voluntary scrubbing of the floor in the midst of party preparations. Keep your lip zipped.

I called Judge Reyes again, felt mildly guilty that I was going sailing instead of sticking around to phone every half hour, and then absolved myself by remembering that Marty was where she was because she'd chosen not to murmur a certain word starting with ''J.''

And then I went on a kid-hunt. Keil was in his room sitting at a computer screen. ''Hi, Keil. Hacking away?''

''Naah. Just playing a game.''

''Want to go for a sail with Julio and Esperanza?''

He spun around in his chair, eyes excited. ''Yeah! I was getting really bored.''

''I'll go find Libby.''

''Oh. She won't want to go.''

I shrugged. ''Then we'll go without her.''

''Grandma won't let me—unless *she* goes.''

I'd forgotten I wasn't in charge. "Okay then," I said. "I'll persuade her."

"She doesn't persuade easy." He sagged in his chair, looking defeated. "She never wants to do anything."

"Get on some warm clothes—it'll be cool on the bay."

"Rebecca, I *live* here." He sounded rude, know-it-all, and obnoxious. The kid was starting to like me.

I went around the house hollering Libby's name until I heard a nasty "What!"

From the TV room. I should have guessed.

"Hi, honey. What's on?"

No answer.

"Keil and Esperanza and I are going for a sail—want to come?"

No answer.

I stepped between Libby and the TV. "Libby, is something wrong, honey?" I could have bitten my tongue. Only everything was wrong.

I said, "I just saw your mom. She said to give you her love and tell you she'll be home real soon."

Actually she hadn't, and now that I thought about it, that was another thing that was wrong.

Libby got up and started to walk out of the room. I chugged cabooselike behind her. I said, "Young lady, you answer when I talk to you!"

She turned around and stared at me in shock. But it was nothing compared to the shock I was in. I sounded like my own first grade teacher. The horrid phrase must have been curled up, dormant, in some sort of mental cocoon. In no way did it resemble a butterfly.

Libby picked up a ceramic dish from a table that also held a lamp. She threw it hard and I feinted instinctively, a bad move—better the dish had hit me than the wall, which it did.

"Now look what you've done!" I couldn't believe the sound of my own voice.

''Shithead!'' shouted Libby, and my ears rang as I heard her steps pound up the stairs.

She wasn't kidding. ''Shithead'' about summed it up. I literally couldn't believe the way I was behaving. Some internal trigger had betrayed me. One cross word from a kid and I turned into instant virago. I sat down, shaking, trying to figure out what to do.

Ava came in, wiping her hands on a dishcloth. ''Did I hear profanity coming out of that child's mouth?''

''I'm afraid I made her mad. I'm sorry.''

''Where does she *get* that kind of language?''

''The playground, I guess. All the kids—'' But it wasn't a serious question.

She sat down and looked me in the eye, getting intimate. ''That child is *bad*. Has been from the first day they brought her home. Some kids just come out that way. Wouldn't even nurse, cried all the time, woke up three times every night, screaming like a banshee. It was like she was born with a mission—to drive all the adults out of their minds. When she was four years old, she'd take her bath and leave her panties in the bathroom. Can you imagine that? Four years old and still leaving dirty panties on the bathroom floor! When she was a guest in someone's house!''

''You don't like her, do you?''

Her brown eyes snapped hatred—whether of me or of Libby, I couldn't tell. ''Like her? Whoever heard of not liking a child? She's like her mother, she needs discipline. She needs to have some boundaries set, and know she can't cross them. Of *course* she wouldn't like the person who tries to set them. It's not that I don't like her—that's absurd. Everybody likes children. She doesn't like *me*, Rebecca. No matter what I do, I can't get her to warm up to me. My own granddaughter.''

I was reeling. First from the back-and-forth stances of victim and aggressor, which I'm sure would have taxed a psychotherapist, let alone a mere houseguest. And second, from the concept of Libby's mother needing discipline—Marty, who resembled a calculator more than a human being while waiting for bail to be set. To Marty, that was all it was—waiting for bail, getting over the next hurdle.

I had spent a night in jail once—or most of one—and you never heard such a whining and caterwauling. I like to think of myself as no more neurotic than the average, but at the time, I was worried I'd get a venereal disease from the blankets on my bunk. Being in jail brings out the terrified child in you—unless, of course, you've been "disciplined" out of most of your emotions.

I was willing to bet Marty had not only picked up her dirty panties, but rinsed them and mended the lace by age four. After that she'd probably earned enough washing dishes and setting tables to buy new ones in case they wore out from too much scrubbing. And still she couldn't appease this great maw of judgment and censure.

I stood up, feeling slightly queasy. "I'd like to take the kids sailing with a friend. Do you think you could clear off a space in the kitchen so I can make a snack for us?"

I was truly shocked at the edge to my voice. I needed to get along with this woman—she had the power to throw me out of here, and for some stubborn (probably not too healthy) reason, I very much wanted to stay right now, to see the thing through, at least till Marty was released. I had the sinking feeling of wanting desperately to help, and that frightened me, seemed inappropriate; this family had been muddling through one way or another before I came along. Who was I to play rescuer? Yet I was getting caught up in the role. And I wasn't going to be effective if I didn't stop offending Ava.

But I needn't have worried. The snapping eyes had lost their focus; she was tearing up. "I guess I picked another 'inappropriate' time." There was fury in her voice, but it was the frustrated rage of defeat. She was handing the power over.

I simply couldn't believe it. Instead of using that giant head of energy she'd just worked up, she'd gone all victimized and soft. Or so it seemed. Why didn't I trust it?

Deliberately I made my voice calm and lawyerlike. "Not at all. Is there tuna fish? Maybe I could make some sandwiches. We could stop and get some potato chips and Cokes."

"Marty doesn't let them have sugar."

"Juice then. It *is* all right with you if they go?"

She shrugged, still mad. "I guess you're in charge here. I usually don't let one go without the other. And Libby shouldn't be allowed to go until she apologizes for using filthy language."

"But if one can't go without the other, that would penalize Keil."

She turned toward the kitchen, big shoulders heaving again. "That'll just be on her conscience, won't it?"

I went up and found Libby. "Your grandma said you couldn't go sailing until you apologized for calling me a shithead."

"I don't give a shit who I called a shithead. I told you I didn't want to go sailing, shithead."

I laughed and hit her with a pillow. "What'd you call me?"

"SHITHEAD!!!!"

I cupped my ear and whispered, "Could you say that again, please?"

"Shithead!"

"Oh. I thought you said *cabeza de mierda.*"

"What's that?"

"Shithead in Spanish. Esperanza taught it to me."

She laughed, caught herself having fun, and put her hand over her mouth. "She did not! She never swears."

"You're right, she didn't. But I did see her this afternoon.

Her dad took me to talk to her because she's real, real upset about something.''

"Sadie." Libby looked down at her coverlet and found a design to trace.

"It isn't just that, honey. It's something about a white thing. Do you know what it is?''

She looked up, interested for the first time. "A white thing?''

"Uh-huh. She said it looked like a brain.''

"A brain? She told *you* that?''

"Yes. Have you seen it?''

"Maybe. Why'd she tell *you* about it?''

"Kids like me. Haven't you noticed?''

She threw the pillow back at me. "Shithead.'' But there was no venom in the word.

"See? You hardly know me and already you gave me a nickname.''

"Is Esperanza *really* upset?''

"Really, really upset.''

"Really, really, really upset?''

It went on like that for a few more exchanges, while Libby let me know she wouldn't dream of going except that Esperanza needed her so desperately. But I knew the battle was won the first time I mentioned the white thing—I couldn't tell whether she knew what it was, but she obviously didn't know why it was upsetting Esperanza. And she was burning up with curiosity.

Keil the Wonder Child already had the sandwiches made. How he knew we were even going, much less that we needed tuna sandwiches, I had no idea. Maybe he was psychic; he seemed to know what you wanted half the time when you didn't know yourself.

Julio kept his boat at the marina, and we were to meet him there at three. We'd have just made it if the phone hadn't rung. Keil answered it—who else? "It's for you, Rebecca.''

I snatched the phone, fervently hoping I'd connected with Judge Reyes before I remembered I hadn't been able to leave a message.

"Hello, schweetheart, get me rewrite."

"Rob."

"Hey, what's wrong?"

"Nothing. I was on my way out, that's all. How's—ah—" Where was he? "—Harvard?"

"You don't sound right."

"How'd you know I was here?"

"I tracked you down. The Monterey Bay Aquarium murder is national news, pussycat. Your name was in the *New York Times* this morning."

"Shit!" Guiltily I looked over at Ava.

"I'm getting the weirdest feeling about your attitude."

"Did the paper say Marty's been arrested?"

"Uh-huh. I always thought there was passion beneath that calm exterior."

"And did it mention Don's away in Australia?"

"No. Why?"

"Well, if you recall, they've got two kids."

"Oh, no. You've been elected Mom for a Day? Surely not. Not you."

"I happen to be very good at it," I snapped. "Now, if you'll excuse me, I have some diapers to change."

"Rebecca, you just don't sound like yourself. Are you sure you haven't bitten off more than you can chew?"

"Oh, for heaven's sake, you sound like my mother."

"Nobody sounds like your mother. She's been on the horn as usual, I expect?"

"Actually, yours is the first—uh—call from my old life." I had stopped myself just in time—I'd almost said "unwelcome phone call."

"Your old life? You haven't even been gone twenty-four hours."

Keil and Libby, who had been standing first on one foot and then the other, had taken to whispering and now burst forth in a chorus of ''Anchors Aweigh.''

''Listen, I've really got to go.''

''Have you run away with half a dozen sailors?''

''The kids are trying to remind me in a nice way that we're late for our sailing date.''

''Date? Did you say date?''

''Give me a break, okay? Some kid's dad's taking a bunch of us out on the bay. Could I be excused, please?''

''You really sound harried.''

''That's motherhood for you. 'Bye now.'

''But I didn't tell you what I called for.''

I sighed. ''An exclusive, inside interview, I guess.''

''No.

''No?''

''I wanted to tell you I miss you.''

''That's sweet.''

''I love you.''

Perspiration popped out like a rash on my forehead. I didn't want to hear this. ''Gosh. Well, you're very sweet today. I've got to go, really.''

''Okay. Call you for the story later.''

My hands were as sweaty as my face before he finally let me go. It had been a call from the other side of the moon, so alien was it. I'd let Rob go a long time ago. I just hadn't let myself realize it.

CHAPTER 8

Julio and Esperanza were waiting impatiently beside what Julio said was a Victory, a twenty-one-foot boat in which the five of us were a nice snug fit.

Julio, at any rate, was impatient. Esperanza, I thought, seemed still down in the dumps, though she cheered a little when she saw Libby.

We'd stopped on the way for fruit juice and Cokes, which the kids informed me were usually strictly forbidden, but which, I informed them, were permitted today.

"Okay, who's going to help sail?" asked Julio, looking almost wistfully at Esperanza, clearly wanting her to volunteer.

"Me," said Keil. Of course.

Libby slammed a fist down on the fiberglass deck. "I never get to help."

"You can take turns," I said, but Libby only walloped the boat again.

I could understand her frustration. It must have been tedious having Little Mr. Perfect for a brother. I was starting to get the hang of him a little. He was perfect for the sake of an audience: applauding appreciative adults. Which didn't mean he didn't sincerely think he had to be perfect. In a way, I felt sorrier for him than I did for Libby. At least she knew she was mad and had sense enough to pound on something when she felt like it. I didn't have the feeling Keil had it in him to do that—probably thought it a vulgar display from an inferior and couldn't possibly lower himself.

But I banished the thought as soon as I had it. No doubt he felt judgmental about Libby, but I got the feeling lowering himself didn't come into the picture. He probably just never felt mad and thought anger a curious phenomenon that applied only to other people. Poor baby. I hoped he wouldn't get an ulcer before he was fifteen.

Julio said, "Okay, all kids get into life jackets."

Keil reached under the bow, where they were stowed, but Libby and Esperanza chorused, "Noooo!" in a single agonized howl.

Esperanza, who, like Libby, apparently could get as mad as the next little brat—I mean, the next little darling—said, "Daddy, please! We can all swim!"

Julio hesitated. I got the feeling he'd usually insist, but he looked at the perfect cloudless sky and said, "Okay, I guess we're not going to have a storm. It takes quite a bit to tip one of these babies. But listen, we're not going to make a practice of this; does everybody understand that?"

All three nodded, Keil looking relieved, since he was the only one of the crew who'd actually intended to obey captain's orders, no matter how stupid he'd feel in an orange puffy thing. The girls looked smug, like cats who'd not only just had a dish of cream, but were used to cream, not cat chow.

Julio settled himself at the stern, directing Keil to the bow and us females amidships, if that's what you call the area between front and back. I'd been sailing as often as anyone from Marin County (which is bordered by the San Francisco Bay), but only with experienced sailors who'd done all the work. "Three sheets to the wind" was about all the nautical jargon I knew.

"Okay, Keil," said Julio, "release the jib."

Keil did something or other and Julio gave more orders—

I could have sworn he said something like "Helmsalee," and then "Watch your heads," which even I understood. It meant if we didn't, we'd soon experience the sound effect that goes with the part of a boat called the boom.

We were under way. Blubbery, contented animals were sunning themselves on the breakwater. "Look, kids," I hollered. "Seals."

"Sea lions," said Keil. "They have ears."

Undaunted, excited, I said, "Look. *Baby* seals."

"Rebecca!" said Libby. "Sea lion pups."

Now I was daunted. But impressed. These kids really lived on the bay, really knew what was in their environment. To them, an animal was more than a cat or a rat or an urban raccoon.

Julio must have thought my silence—brought on by city-dweller's envy—meant I felt humiliated by my juniors. Gallantly he came to the rescue. "You kids don't know everything. I bet you don't know what they eat that's really weird."

"At least it's not abalone," said Keil.

Libby hollered, "Keil Whitehead, you shut up! You don't even like abalone."

All that, of course, was a reference to the charge that sea otters ate shellfish that rightfully belonged to humans, an idea that struck me as similar to the notion our ancestors must have held while wresting the Great Plains from the Indians.

Libby, I took it, was a friend of the sea otter.

"You guys know or not?" asked Julio.

"Sea urchins!"

"That's not so weird. Otters eat them."

Keil said, "Otters eat everything."

"Shut up!" Libby smacked him.

I pretended nothing had happened, sure Keil wouldn't do so imperfect a thing as to hit back—but I thought something interesting had been revealed. He wasn't really perfect—he baited his sister. He must be jealous of her.

I sighed at my brilliant deduction. Of course he was jealous of her. They were siblings.

"Their teeth turn purple," said Libby, now recovered. "And so do their bones. From eating urchins."

I looked to Julio for confirmation. "Well, lavender, anyway," he said. "Doesn't anyone want to know about sea lions?"

Libby said, "I do! I do!"

"They eat rocks. I mean, they swallow them. You can't digest a rock, can you?" He nudged Esperanza gently, and obediently she shook her head. But she remained expressionless, not participating.

"Sometimes their stomachs contain as many as a hundred rocks."

"Ew. Gross!" said Libby.

I was curious. "What are the rocks for?"

"No one knows."

Keil said, "Maybe they're for ballast."

I laughed at his witticism, but Julio said, "That's one of the theories."

We caught the wind and were soon far out on the bay. I was getting spray in my face and loving it. Esperanza, showing faint signs of revival, dangled first fingers, then toes. She had to turn around to dangle her toes, which made Julio murmur once again about a life jacket, but his protest was half-hearted. I could tell the last thing he wanted to do at the moment was interfere with anything she might actually be enjoying.

Most kids, I thought, would give anything to be in that position for an afternoon. He'd probably let her eat candy bars and fries if she asked for them.

Libby wasn't letting her off so easy. "A shark'll bite you."

"There aren't any sharks in the bay—are there, Daddy?"

"Sure. Leopard sharks."

"But they don't bite."

"Blue sharks now and then. They won't bite your toes, though. Or if they do, they'll probably only eat one. They don't think humans taste very good."

"Daddy!" Esperanza looked mad. She probably hated being teased.

"No kidding. They usually only take one bite and then they go, 'Ptui!' and swim away. And when they bite, they usually go for divers wearing wet suits, because they look like seals. Sharks can't see too well."

"Yeah, but they can really smell," said Keil. "They can smell one part of blood in a hundred million parts of water. I thought that was so rad, I memorized it."

Libby hit him again. "Oh, they cannot! They can't even count that high."

As adults will at such moments, Julio and I sought out each other's eyes and shared a smile. The moment lasted a little longer than it should have. I found myself slightly embarrassed, yet unable to break away.

Libby said, "Didn't anyone think that was funny?"

We dropped anchor for a while, off Lovers Point, and ate our sandwiches, throwing scraps to the sea gulls that circled relentlessly, though the kids said I even had their name wrong—they were western gulls; you could tell by their white heads.

Anything I might think about the name of the point was probably mistaken, too, Keil informed me. It took its name from the Lovers of Jesus Church.

Esperanza seemed to get quieter now, retreating back to her shell. She didn't eat a thing.

Libby, as if to compensate, got more rambunctious and demanding. She would grab Julio's arm and shake it. "I want to see *otters*, Julio." Whining the word "otters."

"How about if I eat my sandwich first?"

"No-o-o. You love fish, you shouldn't be eating tuna."

"You're not kidding I love them. I'm crazy about tuna. And sharks—I bite them, they don't bite me. And sushi. Especially sushi."

"Ew. Gross!"

"Thar she blows!" hollered Keil.

"A whale?" Even I knew there wouldn't be whales in these waters in August, but what else could he mean?

For once, he didn't bother to correct me, just shrugged and gave us all a cute grin. "No, otters. There isn't an otter yell."

"Where? Where?" Libby nearly capsized the boat trying to see them.

"Over there." He pointed off to the right, toward the far shore. "I think it's several rafts. What do you think, Julio?"

Edge of hand to forehead like an old sea dog, Julio scanned the scenery. He shrugged. "I don't know. There's something out there. Maybe it's just kelp."

"Let's go," Libby begged. "Julio, let's go, let's go."

He retrieved the anchor and once again told Keil to release the jib.

There were three dark spots up ahead that could be rafts of otters, and I found myself nearly as excited as Libby at the prospect of seeing them up close. These furry critters have been known to amuse tourists by playing Frisbee with old hubcaps. Even when behaving less anthropomorphically, the California sea otter is the cutest mammal in the water, and doesn't have that much competition on land.

"Damn!" Keil said. "I think it's kelp."

Julio stared long and critically. "There goes one." Some of the kelp had taken a dive. "It's kelp *and* otters. Crazy little things. They like to wrap up in kelp blankets."

"For warmth? You'd think there'd be a better way."

"No, to anchor themselves. They have a hell of a time keeping warm, though, even with those beautiful coats."

"No blubber," said Keil.

Julio nodded. "Awkward stage of evolution. They have to keep their fur full of air—which takes up about ten percent of their time, if you can imagine that—and they have to keep their paws out of the water; and then, of course, they have to consume all those calories that people get so bent out of shape about."

"Look!" Libby shouted. "They're eating."

Otters are terribly trusting little animals, which is one reason they became nearly extinct in the nineteenth century and the early part of this one. I read somewhere that in 1900 a single otter pelt went for over one thousand dollars, which must have been nearly enough to retire on in those days. Protective legislation was finally enacted, but the otter, though apparently a very bright little animal, never got smart enough to be afraid of people. By now, these rafts had let us come close enough to see how zany they looked with their fur half-wet. When soaked, a sea otter is sleek as a seal, but let him start to dry out, and his fine fur—the thickest of any mammal in the world—goes every which way.

The ones Libby had spotted—probably having their eighty-ninth snack of the day—were lying on their backs, reclining Romans at a banquet. They were using rocks to bang away at shellfish, setting up a fairly clamorous racket. For thumbless beasts, they use their paws a lot like we do.

Julio said, "We don't give them shells in their tank at the aquarium. It's cute to watch them show their tool-using skills, but you have to pay. They take the shells and bang them against the windows like a bunch of teenage vandals. The acrylic gets so scarred-up, you can't even see through it. Know how much it costs to feed one of those critters? About six thousand dollars a year."

It was hard to imagine these cute little devils as vandals. Their perennially worried expressions made them look responsible.

"They like to raft with the same sex," said Julio. "Those are females."

Only I was brave enough to ask the question: "How can you tell?"

The kids looked alarmed.

He pointed: "They have pups. Also, some of them have crummy-looking noses. When they mate, the mate bites the female's nose."

"Oh, no. Spousal violence."

"Well, I guess he needs something to hang on to."

I considered, and found myself more or less thinking aloud. "Come to think of it, it's not the easiest thing to do . . . in a swimming pool, say."

As if by signal, Libby and Esperanza clapped their hands over their ears. "EEEEEEWWWWWW! Gross!"

Even Keil looked a little undone.

I probably blushed; I certainly shrank against the side of the boat, horrified that I'd shocked these innocent children.

But Julio only laughed; in fact, couldn't seem to stop laughing. "They do that to me all the time. Remember the good old days? When it was the kids who had to watch their language?"

Libby said, "I don't see any pups," which neatly changed the subject.

The pups were discovered and admired, and Julio treated us to lore about what good moms sea otters are (though they're pretty indifferent dads), and also told us more about the criminal tendencies of the little gonifs. Not only are they window-scratching vandals, they aren't above stealing food from each other, even knowing it costs their pals several dives and hard work with a rock to snare a tender morsel. The worst part is that one of the prime times for robbery is the third or fourth day of a courtship, when the romance begins to pall.

Hearing that kind of made me proud to be a human being.

I'd rather have to listen to ''I'll call you tomorrow'' than watch my so-called sweetie swim away with my hard-earned clams.

Libby and Keil asked a million questions about everything except mating habits, and I contributed quite a few myself, but Esperanza, if anything, seemed to sink deeper into herself. Julio tried to stay upbeat, but I could see him glancing at her now and then, brow furrowed. Finally he looked at the sky and said it was time to go home. Predictably, Libby and Keil howled.

Esperanza, unless I was mistaken, looked relieved. I though she must have agreed to come for Julio's sake, playing parent to her own father. Her mood had her like a starfish, sucking at its prey with relentless tube feet.

On the way back, Libby was permitted to change places with Keil, be Julio's cocaptain. There was a good breeze. The sails puffed prettily and we glided peacefully, in one of those rare blissful intervals when everything goes right and I understand why people love sailing so much. Esperanza's toes still trailed, kicking up little bits of white foam. And then she was gone.

Libby screamed. Julio moved so quickly I could barely follow his actions, but in retrospect, I think he must have done this: released the mainsail, crossed to the bow, popped off the jib, hollered, ''Life jackets!'' and dived overboard. I think Keil was gone even before Julio. I was too stunned to stop him, even to notice he was about to jump.

I was trying to take in what had happened, that Esperanza had simply shoved herself in with a little push of her arms, as if dropping from the side of a pool. She had done it so fast, I wasn't aware of movement until she was already in the water. Keil and Julio had moved nearly as fast. And now Libby was moving, leaning under the bow, coming up with orange life jackets, throwing them overboard. Somebody grabbed one—Keil, I thought—and I grabbed the tiller so as to be doing something, anything at all. But the boat didn't seem to be moving much, drifting slightly with the wind, that was all.

I held my breath as Keil struggled into his life jacket and caught the other two. Both Julio and Esperanza had disappeared.

I watched, heart pounding in my throat and making it close, as Keil got farther away. Though we weren't moving much, he seemed to be floating downwind with the swells.

Julio was never going to find her, not in that murk.

He surfaced. I let my breath out. He looked like a mother otter, pup tight to her chest. It had to be Esperanza he held, though I'd never have recognized her. Tangled in kelp, she resembled the spawn of a sea monster. She was struggling, trying to get away. But then I saw it wasn't that—she was coughing.

I was paralyzed. I couldn't stand to watch, but couldn't pull my eyes away. Keil swam to the other two and helped Julio get Esperanza into her jacket. She wriggled like an eel, trying to breathe and stay afloat at the same time. Julio kept hollering, "Relax! Relax, *Nena*!" which might have made me smile if I hadn't been so scared. Relax. Oh, sure, Dad, no problem, two seconds out of a watery grave.

My breath caught. They weren't out yet. How was I supposed to sail the damn boat over to them?"

The thought seemed to hit Julio at the same time.

"Grab the tiller."

Great. I was holding it so tight my knuckles were white.

"Pull in a little bit."

Huh? How did you pull a boat in? A car, no problem, but where was the ignition on this baby?

He hollered something else. Pull my shit in? Was this some Chicano expression meaning "Don't panic"?

Libby's voice was strong, almost authoritative: "Pull your sheet in, Rebecca."

Oh, my sheet. He must mean sail. But how did you pull a sail, and what was in? On land, you pulled *into* a parking place; was there a nautical equivalent?

Libby said, "Grab the line—that's your sheet. Pull it. Catch it in the cam-cleat."

What line? And what was a cam-cleat? But I didn't ask aloud. Things were bad enough.

Line must mean rope. The same rope Julio had popped off before he'd jumped. It had to be that. It was the only thing I could reach. Ah, and he must have popped it out of a little lock, which might be a cam-cleat; if I could just reverse the procedure . . .

I fumbled till Libby said, "Good."

"Libby, can you sail?" It hadn't occurred to me.

"You're going to have to jibe!" Julio yelled.

Dear God, I was going to have to *what*?

Libby said, "Rebecca? Could you take the jib?"

Jib? Jibe? Were they the same thing? I'd thought jib was the little sail on the bow.

"I took sailing lessons last summer."

Julio yelled, "Fill up your sails! Fill up your sails!" His voice was none too gentle.

Just how the hell do you do that, Mr. Julio Goddamn Captain Bligh? I'd be delighted to fill up my sails if you could be bothered to let me know what the fuck you're talking about.

Libby, apparently sick and tired of not being heard, started yelling, too, right in my face, "I can do it, Rebecca! Give me the tiller! Go to the bow! Take the jib."

Yes. The jib *was* that little sail. Everyone knows what a jib is; I wasn't that dumb. "Take the jib" had to mean grab the little rope—I meant sheet—and pull it in or let it out or something.

"Wrap the sheet around the winch."

Winch?

I winced.

"Okay, we're going to jibe now. Watch out. Watch out! Rebecca, watch your head!"

The boom went boom on the back of my skull. How were you supposed to watch your own head anyway?

For a few minutes Libby struggled to get into the right reach, or whatever you call it, while Julio was occupied with getting himself and Keil wrapped around Esperanza, putting her in the middle of a huddle, as is recommended for hypothermia.

Seeing what he was doing reminded me how cold the water was, and how fast a child can succumb to it. With the communications problem, I doubted I'd have been able to handle the boat alone—I only hoped Libby could do it.

Again, Julio began shouting instructions. Libby, brow furrowed, would nod to show she understood, and would let me know if she needed help from me, remembering, unlike Julio, to translate the jargon. But I didn't feel very helpful. Mostly I sat there, tense from toes to ears, feeling stupid and useless and hoping against hope.

We missed them on the first pass, by about six feet. But now we were close enough for Libby to hear better, for her and Julio to work more closely together, and on the second pass we nearly ran over them. Keil had to put a hand out to shove us out of the way. Libby said, "Pop the jib, Rebecca."

Right. Remove the sheet from the cam-cleat. I could handle it.

She popped the mainsheet, and we stalled out, luffing in the wind.

Julio handed me a limp, glassy-eyed Esperanza. She was shivering like a malaria victim and her lips were blue. She felt a little stiff. Automatically I started to rub her bare arms.

But Julio, boosting Keil over the side, still had one eye on his child. "Don't massage her, Rebecca. Take off her PFD. Hold her close to your body."

"PFD?" Was the jargon ordeal ever going to be over?

Libby was helping Keil in. "Life jacket."

"But PFD?"

Keil said, "Personal flotation device."

Oh. Of course. Did they think I was mentally deficient? By now I had it off and I'd draped an extra sweatshirt I'd brought around her shoulders. I couldn't get her arms into it. They wouldn't move easily.

Julio climbed in and took the tiller. Keil had taken off his own PFD and was sitting, back straight, trying like hell to be brave, holding his elbows and shivering nearly as badly as Esperanza. His lips were also blue.

"Libby, hug Keil," said Julio.

"Ewwww. Gr—"

"Do it."

Keil said, "No. Let her huddle with Esperanza and Rebecca."

Julio hesitated. If the three of us formed a huddle, Esperanza's body heat would return much more quickly. Almost visibly, I saw him shake off the impulse to agree. It would leave Keil with no help.

"Shut up and do what I say!"

Libby put her arms around him, but she wouldn't press tight against him and he wouldn't hold her close, soak up her warmth.

Julio said, "Dammit, sit in his lap. Keil, hold her like a baby—up close."

Libby said, "Yuck. That's incest."

"You two are the worst sailors I ever saw."

That did it. They snuggled up.

Expertly, Julio sailed the Victory back to her slip, shivering himself, his own lips turning blue.

CHAPTER 9

We'd come in Marty's car because there was more room in it. Libby knew about a blanket in the trunk, the one that had been there since the time she had appendicitis and they wrapped her in it at the doctor's office and sent her directly to the hospital. Her mom was going to take it back to the doctor one day, but we could use it now for Esperanza.

Somehow the high-pitched chatter was comforting as I wrapped the soaked child, who seemed as bony and vulnerable as a wet kitten. She leaned heavily against me, cuddling up in a way that let me know she wanted comfort and she was glad to be alive and intended to stay that way. Her fursoft eyes were pleading, but what they wanted, I hadn't the least idea.

Julio had to tie up the boat, though he said he'd come back later to take the sails down. He was going to meet us at Marty's, where, despite Ava's witchy presence, we'd decided to go—it was more cheerful than his house, and more important, it had two bathrooms, which were what we needed most right now.

I put the three kids in the back, in a hypothermia huddle, Esperanza in the middle. Though Libby and Keil were silent now, I felt them. I knew what was going on with them. Libby was all right, she was excited, she didn't begin to comprehend what had happened, that Esperanza might have died. It was almost an adventure to her. Keil was deeply ashamed at having jumped in without thinking, having needed to be rescued himself.

I said, "You kids are heroes, you know that? It was pretty amazing what you both did."

I didn't know if it was the right thing to say or not. It certainly didn't come from the heart. Libby, the so-called difficult one, had truly saved the day, and I wanted to give her the praise she was due. Clearly everyone, including me, had seriously underestimated her. It made me sad to think how stories get started about people—they take on a role first in the family and then in the world—and we just keep believing the stories instead of seeing the real person. It was pretty hard to believe any ten-year-old, much less one who everyone seemed to think was a big baby, could have performed so beautifully in an emergency. Libby was no baby. She was a kid who had a bad rap—and she was obviously one of those people who came into her own under pressure. Maybe she'd end up a brain surgeon.

As for Keil, I wanted to tell him it nearly broke my heart watching him try to be a grownup and the best little boy in the world and now Superboy, and that he didn't have to be any of that, but I didn't think he'd believe me.

So I ended up doing what all adults probably did—giving him strokes for doing the stuff that was standing between him and being a kid, his own kid, not everybody's perfect image of a kid.

It truly *was* amazing what he'd done. Amazingly stupid. He could have been killed. And amazingly unnecessary. And astonishingly inappropriate. But here I was praising it. And even that wasn't good enough for Keil.

He mumbled, "I didn't do anything."

"Hit him, will you, Libby?"

"I can't. He's too wet."

"Oh, Keil, you must be freezing."

"I'm fine." His teeth were chattering. I found the heater,

turned it on, and drove silently, contemplating the unimaginable—that a much-loved kid like Esperanza could have problems so large she wanted to die.

Marty's door was opened by a scared-looking Ava. "Esperanza fell in," I said, racing past her, and no one contradicted me. Libby and I took her in the bathroom and put her under a warm shower, clothes and all, while Keil showered in his mother's bathroom. Libby found some sweats for Esperanza, and her mother's terry cloth robe for Julio to wear, while Ava dried their clothes in the Maytag.

While Julio showered, I went down and made Esperanza some bouillon with a chicken-flavored cube, telling myself it wasn't really chicken soup and I wasn't being silly, you were supposed to drink hot liquids for hypothermia, and feeling like my own mother. By this time, Ava had changed Libby's sheets and made Esperanza get in bed.

Before I took the cup up, I had a little conference with Keil. It was agreed that for a mere $7.50, Trap Door would find a way to get Ava out of the house and keep her out for the next hour, while we all recovered.

As I mounted the stairs, I heard his panicked-sounding voice: "Grandma, could you take me to the drugstore? We haven't got a thermometer, and we have to make real sure Esperanza's temperature doesn't go down."

I couldn't hear what Ava answered, but the next thing he said was, "Rebecca dropped it." The boy was resourceful, no question about it.

Esperanza was sitting up on a pile of pillows, hair still wet, but otherwise looking almost normal.

"A little soup?"

She frowned, involuntarily, I was sure—she hadn't Libby's bent for candor.

"You don't like soup?"

"It's okay."

"Hot chocolate?"

"Yeah!" She smiled. Really smiled.

Libby smiled, too, wistfully. "Me, too?"

"Sure."

I practically fell all over myself—and did dribble soup—getting back downstairs, only to find a problem at the bottom—in the form of unexpected guests at the door. It was Warren Nowell and a woman, bearing a fat-humped platter covered in aluminum foil. Still holding the cup, I let them in.

Warren was dressed in a polo shirt and white pants. The woman wore a wrap-around skirt and simple pink blouse. She looked a few years older than he, but her hair was gray and I thought perhaps it had turned prematurely. "Hello, Ms. Schwartz." His voice was smooth. "This is my wife, Mary Ellen."

"Please come in."

"We brought you a ham. We thought with the kids and all, you might not have time to cook."

I was trying to make appropriate noises and figure out how to take the ham while holding the cup of bouillon and also how to get rid of them without being rude when Julio bellowed, "Hey, Rebecca, do we have any hair conditioner?"

It's possible I blushed. I smiled sheepishly at the Nowells while Libby hollered, "There's a new batch in the cabinet."

I led them into the kitchen. "That's Julio Soto. I'm afraid we're having a little crisis around here at the moment. He took us sailing and his daughter fell overboard. Both he and Keil went in after her, and everyone's still trying to get warm and calm down.

"I was just going to make Esperanza some hot chocolate and pour myself a glass of wine. Will you join me?"

"We'd love to," said Mary Ellen, but I thought Warren looked unhappy. She kept talking as I poured their wine and then took milk out of the fridge and poured it into a pan.

"You know, the board met this afternoon and voted Warren acting director."

"That's wonderful," I said absently. "Congratulations."

"Thank you." She handed me a box of chocolate—I hadn't even heard her looking for it—and I wondered where she'd found it. I was so befuddled, it took me a moment to realize she, not Warren, had accepted my thanks.

"We're really going to miss Sadie. You can't know what a wonderful person she was."

Julio padded in, barefoot, the robe knotted around him. He held his arms open in a model's gesture. "You think pink is my color? Oh—Warren. Mary Ellen."

Mary Ellen said, "It's all right. Rebecca explained about Esperanza."

He nodded, undaunted, and continued full speed ahead. "Warren, boy, I thought you hated Chardonnay."

"Mary Ellen wanted some."

Mary Ellen said, "You didn't want wine, Warren? Why didn't you say so?"

Libby came in. "Where's the hot chocolate?"

"Coming up," I said. "Want to take it upstairs?"

She spoke softly, as if her feelings were hurt. "I'll drink mine down here."

That was puzzling. I looked my question at Julio, thinking he must have popped into his daughter's room on the way down. "Esperanza's gone quiet again," he said.

"I'll take it up." I was glad to get away. Mary Ellen had reminded me a little of Lady MacBeth, with her take-charge manner and her proud talk of Warren's ascendancy. I shivered a little at the analogy—there was a spot of blood on someone's hand, and it was someone capable of jamming a letter opener into a person's eye. Mary Ellen might have the stuff, I thought.

Esperanza had the covers over her head.

"Hot chocolate!" I sang out merrily, as if I hadn't noticed a thing.

She peeked out, letting me see she'd been crying.

"Can we talk?" I said.

No answer.

"Honey, you learned something in the bay today. I know you did. I felt it when I was holding you on the boat."

"What?"

"That you don't want to die. That's right, isn't it?"

"I guess so."

"Sit up and drink." I offered the cup.

She took it and settled herself on the pillows. When she had sipped a little, I said, "You can tell me about it, really, honey. You know why? Because you're my client. Have you ever heard of attorney-client privilege?"

She shook her head.

"Well, it means that whatever you tell me has to be a secret. I'm not allowed to tell anybody unless you tell me I can. If I do, I could be punished by the bar."

"The bar? You mean the place where you drink?"

"No, sweetheart, there's another kind of bar that means a lawyers' professional association. If I told a client's secrets, I could get in big trouble."

She looked at me, sizing me up, deciding whether she was going to hire me. "Are you really a lawyer?"

"Uh-huh."

"Am I really your client?"

"If you want to be, I'm taking your case."

Tears cascaded. She fell against my breast, spilling hot chocolate all over my T-shirt.

"Ouch," I yelled, but I could still hear what she was blubbering: "I don't want to go to jail."

I stroked her hair. "You're not going to jail, honey. Honest. I guarantee it. Do you believe me?"

She sat back and looked in my eyes, assessing. This was

a girl who would do well in business. I think she decided I had an honest face. She nodded.

"Sister Teresa says if you steal something, they put you in jail for it, and *Abuelita*—my grandmother—says you go to hell for it, and Sister Teresa says hell is like jail except you have to stay there forever instead of just forty or fifty years."

"Okay, let's start with hell. Now, not everybody believes in it; we already talked about that."

She nodded.

"But I'm not even sure that people who believe in hell think kids can go there. And the other thing they believe is that you can be forgiven. Remember the two thieves on the cross? That Jesus forgave?"

Her jaw dropped. "How do you know about that? You're Jewish."

"How do you know *that*?"

"Daddy told me. I asked him if he liked you, and he said he did but you probably wouldn't go out with him because he isn't Jewish and you are. Is that true? You aren't prejudiced, are you, Rebecca?"

I told my heart to be still and Esperanza that no, I wasn't prejudiced, but I wasn't sure lawyers could date their clients' fathers. And then I asked my client why she was afraid of her father.

Her gold skin turned almost pale. She whispered, "I told him I found it on the beach."

"The white thing? You told him that about the white thing?"

She stared at her feet. "I lied. I stole it."

"And you're afraid he'll punish you?"

"Yes. I'm afraid he'll be so mad, he'll send me back to Santa Barbara, and *Abuelita* will tell Sister Teresa, and I don't know what she'll do! She might turn me in to the police and get me sent to jail."

I smiled. "She can't hurt my client. I don't know whether

kids can go to hell or not, but I guarantee you they can't go to jail.''

"They can't?'' She looked utterly unbelieving. "But Sister says—''

"Sister's wrong. But don't worry. Your dad's not going to send you back.''

She was alarmed. "You won't tell him, will you?''

I must have looked flustered. She'd caught me in a conflict of interest. I had a responsibility to let her parent know that nothing was seriously wrong—nothing by adult standards, that is. Didn't I?

"You promised! Attorney-client privilege.''

That settled it. My responsibility lay with my client.

"Of course I won't tell him. No problem. Now tell me about the white thing. You know, the law distinguishes between different kinds of stealing. There's petty theft and grand theft, for instance. Between you and me, legally petty theft isn't much of a crime. Of course, morally's another matter, but I'm your lawyer, and the law isn't allowed to get into moral questions. Now, even if they sent kids to jail—which they don't, I can't make that clear enough—what you did isn't the same as stealing a car, say. That would be grand theft, and a grownup might get a few years for that, but—'' I shrugged "—a random white thing probably isn't worth very much.''

About halfway through this speech, a change started to come over her face. I thought it was just worry, but it had congealed into misery by the time I finished.

Her voice trembled. "What if it is worth a lot?''

This was getting frustrating. "Darling, do you think you could tell me what it is?''

"I'm not *sure* what it is. That's why I gave it to Sadie. So she could tell me.''

"Well, what does it look like? Besides a brain, I mean? What do you *think* it is?''

She was very solemn. "A pearl of great price."

"Ah. It must be a freshwater pearl. Those are the ones with little wrinkles—like convolutions in a brain."

She shook her head. "My mom has a necklace made out of freshwater pearls. They look more like Rice Krispies than brains. This one's different. It's not very round either, but it's more like a rock—and it's a *whole* lot bigger."

"How big?"

"A little smaller than a golf ball."

"It couldn't be a pearl then, honey. Pearls don't come that big."

"Oh, yes, they do. I did a report on them." There was authority in her voice. She straightened her spine and began to recite. "The largest pearl ever found was called the Pearl of Allah. It weighed fourteen pounds. A native from an island found the humongous white thing on the inside of a giant clam. The only problem was, the clam closed both of its shells while he was looking at it, which killed him. That was in 1934."

She was adorable, but I had to laugh. I was utterly charmed out of my mind, and laughing my head off. I couldn't understand why she'd stopped and purposefully furrowed the spot between her brows, disapproval personified.

"You don't believe me!" If she'd been standing, she'd have stamped her foot.

"I do, I do, it's not that at all. I'm laughing because you're so cute."

She summoned every bit of her ten-year-old dignity. "I *prefer* to be taken seriously."

"But I do take you seriously. It's just that my boyfriend—"

"Your boyfriend!"

I could see the idea distressed her. "My ex-boyfriend does exactly what you're doing, that's all. Only he's out of school, so he doesn't write reports. He's a newspaper reporter. He writes news stories and then quotes himself. He's very cute when he does it, too.''

"Oh." Still hurt. But I was touched by the way she hated the boyfriend talk. She really wanted me to go out with her dad. Oh, well. It was an odd thing to do for a client, but if she insisted—

She said sullenly, "It was an *oral* report. I was *supposed* to memorize it."

"Could I hear the rest of it?"

"I guess so." She drew up her spine again. And suddenly I saw a chance to make points.

"Hold it a minute. I'll teach you something. Want to see how a lawyer makes the jury listen? When you talk to me, make me vibrate."

"Huh?"

"*Imagine* you're making me vibrate. It's a trick for projecting your voice." (Naturally, I didn't mention I'd learned this, not at Clarence Darrow's knee, but in my acting class.)

"Two years after the horrible tragedy," she resonated, "a man who came to the island cured the chief's son of a terrible disease, so the chief gave him the pearl. The man was an American. But the chief told the man he shouldn't ever sell the pearl, or a great catastrophe would strike his family."

I vibrated like crazy on "catastrophe."

"So naturally the man kept the pearl, which was known far and wide ever after as the biggest pearl in the whole world. He could never sell it even though in 1971—no, I think it was 1972—no, '71. In 1971 the Guinness Book of World Records said it was worth four million dollars." Her stage presence dissolved. "You think that puts it in the grand theft category?"

"Whew. I'd say so. But, sweetheart, you didn't steal the Pearl of Allah, did you?"

"No, but I bet the one I got is worth plenty. I mean if it

is a pearl. Whoever heard of a pearl as big as a Ping-Pong ball?''

''Just about nobody, I guess. So where did you get this pearl of great price?'' I tried to keep my voice casual.

She pleated the coverlet. ''From Ricky.''

''Ricky? The model-maker?''

''I was going to put it back! I was always going to put it back!''

''Okay, take it easy, honey. Just tell me what happened, and you'll feel better, I promise.''

She kept looking at her ever-smaller pleats. All she gave me to look at was the top of her head.

''Well, Amber and I wanted to play Ping-Pong, but there weren't any balls. And she had to go to the bathroom, so she told me there were some balls out in the garage. I found this paper bag with six-packs in it—you know what they look like? They're like a piece of cardboard and then a plastic thing on the balls.''

''You mean plastic with little pockets? Like the way they package small toys?''

''Uh-huh. Only one of them had a ball in it that wasn't a ball. I only noticed because I pulled it out first. It didn't feel right. It was heavy.'' Finally she looked up, wanting to make contact. ''I saw a picture of the Pearl of Allah when I was doing my report. You know why it's called that?''

I shook my head.

''It's supposed to look like Mohammed's turban. But it really looks just like a brain. And so did this one. There it was, just lying there, in my hand. *Looking exactly like the Pearl of Allah!* Only smaller.''

Her eyes were shining with treasure-lust; she wouldn't be the first person to have had a sudden criminal impulse regarding a great gem. ''I wanted to have it for a little while.''

''I know, honey.''

''I asked Sadie if it was real, and she said she'd have to do some research on it, and then—she got *killed*! What if it really is real and somebody found out she had it and they killed her for it?''

I decided to confront her fear head-on: "It wouldn't be your fault, honey. It wouldn't, wouldn't, wouldn't! Do you believe me?''

She nodded, looking down.

"No, you don't. That's really why you wanted to drown, wasn't it? Because you think that?''

The small head bent once more.

"And that's why you sent your dad back to get the pearl— I mean, the white thing. Because if it were in Sadie's desk, or her house, then that would mean she couldn't have been killed for it. Right?''

"Uh-huh.''

"Okay, I'll find out.''

"You will?''

"Somehow or other, I will.''

"And you won't tell anybody?''

That was another matter. "Not tonight. I can promise you that much.''

"You said you wouldn't tell anybody, ever! You said you could get in trouble with the bar.''

Okay. All right, already.

"Well, I did and I won't. But I want to give you a chance to sleep on it. Maybe things will look different in the morning, and you'll feel like talking the whole thing over with your dad by then. Could you think about that?''

"I guess so.''

"There's one other thing that worries me. Did you tell Amber about the white thing?''

"No.''

"Why do you think she's grounded?''

She spoke reluctantly. "I think Ricky thinks she took it.''

"Don't you think we need to get her off the hook?''

Tears spilled out of her eyes. "Oh, Rebecca, she'll never be my friend again!"

"Sure she will." But I thought she'd gone as far as she could for one night. "Listen, let's talk more about it in the morning, shall we?" I patted her leg.

"Okay. Could you send Libby up now?"

Her face was completely innocent of worry. If confession is good for the adult soul, it's a positive transfusion for the youthful one. The idea that this girl, now ready to play Barbies with her friend, had tried to kill herself that afternoon seemed ridiculous.

Her dad, on the other hand, was now looking ready to take his own life. He also looked pretty silly sitting on Marty's terra-cotta sofa in her short pink robe, and I thought he must surely be uncomfortable entertaining guests that way. But Mary Ellen's voice floated everything else out of my consciousness:

"Warren wanted to quit, you know—" Julio had found peanuts, and she took a handful"—but I hate a quitter. I said, 'Warren, you have to make your own opportunity.' "

Warren's face couldn't have looked more pinched if his nose had been caught in a vise. Mary Ellen swallowed the handful of peanuts, looking as if they satisfied her like a multiple orgasm. "And I was right. Good things happen to people with gumption, people who stick it out no matter what." She was on her second glass of wine.

I said, "Warren, I didn't know you were unhappy at the aquarium."

He looked bewildered and a bit rabbity. "I—uh—wasn't."

"Warren, you were! You knew you'd never go to the top with Sadie there. She was just too good."

He shrugged, looking apologetic, I thought, though whether for his own sorry self or for his pushy wife, I didn't know. "I wasn't really thinking of 'going to the top.' "

Mary Ellen snorted.

"I've always wanted to write a book," he said wistfully. Julio stood. "I think I'd better get some clothes on."

Warren stood as well. "We won't keep you any longer. We just wanted to make sure Rebecca and the kids didn't need anything." He looked at me, affording Julio an opportunity to slip out. "Is there anything else we can do for you?"

He was the perfect picture of an acting director, a person who has achieved seniority taking care of the also-rans—in Marty's case, more than an also-ran. A possible serious loser.

"No, thanks." I started to walk toward the door, hoping he and Mary Ellen would take the hint and follow, but Mary Ellen began to gather up wineglasses, a practice I truly hate in a guest. Rather than take her cue and flutter guiltily about in her wake, I continued toward the door.

To my surprise, Warren plucked at my sleeve. "Rebecca, I need to talk to you."

I'm afraid I stared, more or less speechless. He glanced furtively up the stairs. "I didn't know you were involved with Julio."

"I'm not!" The angry, self-justifying words were out before I could stop them, and I was furious at myself for being manipulated into a defensive posture.

"You've got to be careful." He was whispering. "He was at the aquarium last night. I was in the parking lot about seven-thirty. I saw him coming out."

"Warren! Warren, where are you?" Apparently it was her husband whom Mary Ellen had expected to flutter in her wake. She caught up with us before I could ask him what *he* was doing in the parking lot.

CHAPTER 10

I put away the ham and washed the damned wineglasses while Julio got dressed. It was getting on toward six o'clock, and I was thinking of having my long-postponed glass of wine with Julio when he returned—and wondering if it would loosen my tongue enough to tell him what Warren had said.

I tried Judge Reyes again. No answer.

Keil and Ava came in, Keil's step light in his Reeboks, Ava's heavy not so much with weight as with judgment. She carried it in her aura like a coat of mail.

"Rebecca! We got the thermometer!" There was triumph in the boy's voice that had nothing to do with sickroom equipment. Another job well done by Trap Door.

Ava followed him heavily into the back hall, where I met them, dish towel in hand. "Thanks so much, you two, but I don't think we'll need it. She's fine now—Libby's with her."

I could have sworn Ava looked disappointed. Her lips set as she resigned herself to giving up a sick child to nurse. I was trying to handle the implications of that, to deal with the ominous fluttering it made in my gut when Keil hollered, "Rebecca, it's for you!"

I realized the phone had rung and been answered. The receiver clattered on the counter, and the refrigerator door clicked open almost simultaneously.

I was annoyed. The caller, of course, could be only one person, and he'd phoned at an extremely inconvenient time.

"Hello, Rob," I said, making my voice cold enough to raise goose bumps back in Cambridge.

"Rebecca? Is this Rebecca Schwartz? The lawyer?"

"Sorry. I was expecting someone else."

"This is Ricky."

"Who?"

"Ricky Flynn. I met you at Julio's. You're Marty's lawyer, right?"

"Yes. Hi, Ricky."

"Listen, would it be unethical—I mean, would you have a conflict of interest . . . ? Look, I need a lawyer."

"Your three minutes is up," said the operator.

"Ricky, give me your number. I'll call you right back." I'd suddenly realized his voice didn't sound right. This wasn't the cocky Ricky of the morning. This one sounded scared. When I had him on the line again, I said, "Okay, talk slowly. Is this about Sadie?"

"No. It's not. I think someone else is dead."

"You think?"

"Can you meet me in Pebble Beach? Now?"

"Ricky, listen to me. If you're not sure this person's dead, call the police."

He gave me the address and hung up. Damn! Why did the term bimbo apply only to women? Frenzied, I dialed the number Ricky had given me and held my breath. Someone answered on the fifth ring. "Ricky?"

"You want the guy who was just here?"

"Please. It's an emergency."

"Hey!" Whoever it was shouted in my ear. "Hey! Some lady wants you. It's an emergency."

To my surprise, Ricky came back. A good sign. He was behaving like a little boy afraid to defy his mother. If you had to have a kid for a client, it might as well be an obedient one.

"I can't take your case if you're not going to follow instructions."

"Okay. She's dead. I'm sure. I'm certain. Okay?" He sounded more frightened and more childlike with each word. He hung up again, this time resoundingly, now the petulant child. But I believed him. Whoever the woman was, I didn't think anything could be done for her. I hoped my instinct was right.

Ava was hovering, starting to wash the dirty wineglasses. I was sure she'd heard every word, but too bad, I wasn't used to using a kitchen as an office. "Tell Julio I had to go out," I said briskly. I'd memorized the address Ricky gave me, but now I wrote it very deliberately on the memo pad beside the phone. "If you don't hear from me in two hours, call the police and give them this address, will you?"

I hoped that thus being taken into my confidence would discourage her from telling Julio or anyone else what she'd heard—and it would serve as a genuine backup in case Ricky was up to no good. But somehow I wasn't really nervous about that. For all I knew, he had killed the woman he'd called about, but I didn't see him doing any more damage in his current state.

I found him pacing outside a mammoth Spanish-style house, a beautiful house up a long driveway with a gate. The gate had been left open.

Ricky's face was red. I was sure he'd been crying. He was no longer wearing the baseball cap, and he'd changed to fresh jeans and a clean shirt.

"Come," he said, and he led me to a side window, a broken one, broken from the outside, the shards of glass resting on thick carpeting inside. The room was a kind of library, or perhaps a study, lined with books (though many had been tossed on the floor) and furnished with desk and chairs. It was a good, functional workroom and would have been a lovely, restful area as well if it hadn't been for the revolting spectacle of a woman dead on the floor, and the disarray of her fight for her life. A Lhasa apso rose from its post beside the body, trotted to the window, and nearly tore its tiny paws to shreds on broken glass as it tried to climb the wall, barking, snarling, and protecting. "Does she look dead to you?"

"Yes."

"She is. I did a dumb thing."

"Yes?"

"I'm the one who broke the window. She didn't answer the door, and Mellors was barking, back here—that was the funny thing. He should have been up near the front door, where I was. So I came and looked in the window. I saw her like that and—I just didn't think—I broke the window and jumped in. Mellors bit me." He held up his right hand, punctured at the wrist.

I murmured something about a tetanus shot, my mind racing, trying to take it all in.

"She was cold. I think she's been dead a long time."

"Why didn't the alarm go off when you broke the window?"

His boyish face registered utter bewilderment. "The alarm?"

"A house like this must have an alarm. Did you turn it off when you came in?"

"No. My God, if it *had* gone off—"

"And why didn't you phone from here?"

"I panicked. I made sure she was dead and I jumped back out the window—I even forgot to let Mellers out, the library door is shut, that's why he couldn't get to the front—and I got in my car. All I wanted was to get out of there. Pretend it never happened."

"Pretend what never happened?" I was acutely aware I was sounding like Sergeant Jacobson.

He was unfazed. "That she was dead." He let a moment go by, apparently trying once more to assimilate her death.

"But I couldn't go anywhere. I was shaking. I shook for a while, all over, like someone with hypothermia, and finally I cried. And then when I could see, I drove. I don't know where I was going—but I didn't go very far. I guess some adrenaline kicked in or something and I realized I had to report it and that I could be in trouble about the window—and I thought of you. I thought you'd know what to do. Rebecca, did you ever see *Harold and Maude*?"

I gasped. As we talked, we'd been gradually moving away from the window, or more precisely, away from the shrill barking, but I could still see inside. The woman in the room was dressed in white slacks and some kind of pink silky blouse. She looked very slender and she had short blond hair. From the twenty or so paces I was staring from, I could see her cheekbones. Her body was crumpled, her mouth was caught in a grimace, and her head was tilted at a hideous angle; I could see ugly bruises on her neck and a rope or something around it. And yet there was no doubt in my mind she had been elegant—not flashily, ephemerally pretty, but lovely in her bones, as the saying went. She looked about thirty-five. I had assumed from Ricky's distress and—I had to admit—from the dog's name that she and Ricky had been close, but I wasn't prepared for any *Harold and Maude* talk.

"I was in love with her," he said. "I can't believe she's dead. I just can't believe it."

"I don't understand."

He sighed. "I don't guess anyone will. I swear to God, Rebecca! I swear it."

"Take it easy, Rick. I believe you. I don't see why anyone wouldn't be in love with her. She was obviously a very beautiful woman."

And rich.

"She was, wasn't she? But the age difference—people are

sexist about that sort of thing. They just don't want to accept it."

"How old was she?"

He shrugged. "I don't know. Middle fifties, I guess. I'm twenty-nine."

"Well, she looked wonderful. Who was she?"

"Didn't I say? Katy Montebello."

"How do I know that name?"

He shrugged. "It's big around here."

"I remember now. Marty mentioned her. She was a patron of the aquarium."

"That's right. We call it 'sponsor.' "

"So is that how you know her? From the aquarium?"

He nodded.

"Shall we sit on that bench and talk about it? You can tell me the whole story. Then we'll call the police. Okay?"

"You sit. I'll pace." But he seemed relieved that I'd agreed to sit down—had made that much of a commitment to hearing him out. I sat on the white metal bench, more to give him a focus than anything else, and he stood over me, not really pacing much, but occasionally patting his pockets as I'd seen Julio do earlier that day. I could smell a faint odor of alcohol on him.

"You know, I'm a model-maker."

"Yes."

"Well, I do handyman stuff and carpentry and, oh, painting—stuff like that—to keep it together, know what I mean? I'm a sculptor, really. I'd like to devote full time to my art, but I have to make a living." He smiled, sadly, I thought. "I have a little girl."

"Amber."

"Yeah. Amber's mom left me because I could never get my money trip together, and now I have to scramble or I'd never get to see Amber at all—her mom would see to that. At least now I get her weekends and a few weeks in the summer—as long as I can provide a halfway decent place for her to live. So—we all got problems, right?''

''Right.''

''Well, along comes Katy and she sees my work—at the aquarium, I mean, I do a little carpentry there, too—and she wanted me to do some work on her guest house. She has a maid, see, and the maid had to live in the main house, and that cramped Katy's style, so she had me do this work on the guest house—for the maid—and she asked me in to have coffee and drinks and—'' he shrugged ''—she liked me.'' He sounded astonished.

''And you liked her?''

''Umm-HMMMM.'' He swallowed. ''Yeah, I liked her. I liked her a lot.''

''Were you dating?''

''No. No, I wouldn't exactly call it that. But sometimes she'd call and ask me up to have a few drinks. After I finished the carpentry, I mean.''

''And when was that?''

''About three months ago.''

''And would you spend the night?''

''Yeah. I usually would. Or sometimes I wouldn't. We'd drink and we'd have sex and then she'd have someplace else to go. Tonight she asked me to come up early, so maybe she was going out later. I don't know. She said she wanted to talk about something.''

''Frankly, Ricky, it sounds as if she treated you like a servant.''

He stared at the ground.

''Why did you put up with it?''

''I liked her. I was in love with her.'' He looked undecided, as if there was more but he didn't want to get into it. I had a pretty good idea what it was.

''I'm sorry to ask this, but I'm your lawyer and I need to

know what went on. So here's my question: Was there compensation?''

He flushed rosy pink, a nice color to paint a boudoir. ''She'd always say it was for Amber. So I couldn't say no.''

''She gave you money?''

''Yes. Sometimes a fifty, sometimes more. Sometimes nothing.'' He straightened up and looked me in the eye. ''I didn't do it for the money. I would have married her—''

Sure. For the money. ''Other gifts?''

''One.'' He sat on the grass, as if finally defeated. ''She drank a lot. She'd get drunk pretty often and try to give me things. And then about a week ago—I don't know, I think someone dumped her. Someone she cared about, I mean. She got really drunk and started telling me about all the guys she's had—besides her ex-husband, I mean. Oh, man. She named movie stars, politicians, millionaires—practically every dude that ever played in the Crosby. Jeez, it was embarrassing. But, you know, she's got this thing for the sea. We should walk to the other side of the house—'' He stopped, remembering we weren't there on a sight-seeing trip. ''Anyway, this place isn't built right on the ocean for nothing. That's her first love. And she's a big sponsor at the aquarium. She's got a real thing for it, no kidding.''

I nodded.

''So after she dumped her husband—her first husband, I mean, before she married Francis Montebello—some dude came along and wanted to marry her, but he didn't give her a diamond. Uh-uh. He gave her a half-pound pearl.''

My ears pricked up. ''How big?''

''Real big. So big, you couldn't even make jewelry out of it. Anyway, she didn't want to marry the dude, but he said keep the pearl anyway, no one else was good enough for it, or something like that, and so she did. It got kind of famous, at least locally, because she'd show it around and stuff. It's called the Sheffield Pearl, for some reason.''

"I think Marty told me Katy Montebello was once named Katy Sheffield."

"Anyway, she showed it to me one other night. She kept it in a little velvet bag locked in a wall safe. She made this ritual of getting it out and letting me see it and putting it on the glass table and looking at it and I don't know what all—it lasted, seemed like hours."

"She was pretty drunk, huh?"

"Drunk as fifty skunks. And morose. Crying. Awful. Anyway, she gave me the pearl."

"She *gave* you the pearl?"

" 'For Amber.' She said it meant nothing to her and she wanted someone who'd really appreciate it to have it. Well, listen. I was pretty drunk, too."

"Something like that must be worth a lot."

He shrugged. "I don't know. I was going to find out." He tugged at a tuft of grass, pulled up a handful, and pulled up another handful. "Oh, shit!"

I waited.

"I didn't think I should keep it. Thought I'd talk about it with her when we were both sober—and I guess she had second thoughts, too, because that's what she wanted to talk about tonight. That's why she invited me here." He flushed. "To tell you the truth, she left a pretty weird message on my machine. I don't think she remembered giving it to me."

"What did the message say?"

"She asked if I could come over and said the time I should come and all, and then there was this pause and her voice got kind of strange and embarrassed and she said, 'I wonder if you have my pearl?' "

"Oh, Ricky!" It wasn't very professional, but I couldn't keep the dismay out of my voice.

He flushed again. This was a man who shouldn't play poker. "Yeah. Looks bad, huh?"

I shrugged.

"It's true, though. She gave it to me, Rebecca. Think I'd steal a thing like that?"

"Did you bring it?"

He shook his head.

"No? Listen, the message made it pretty obvious she wanted it back. Were you going to pretend she never gave it to you?"

"No!"

I waited, having no choice but to play dumb to protect the anonymity of my other client—the one whose sticky little fingers couldn't be explained by M&Ms.

"I don't have it," he whispered.

"You don't have it?"

"Amber took it. I think she lost it. She won't say what happened to it."

"You're sure she took it? Does she say she did?"

"She denies it, the little witch."

"Why don't you believe her?"

"Where I put it, she had to have taken it. Nobody broke into the house. And anyway, it was like that story about the letter; nobody would have looked for it there. The perfect hiding place. But when I looked for it, it wasn't there."

"Tell me something. Were you still drunk when you hid it?" This was mean of me, but I couldn't stand hearing Amber falsely accused.

"I'm telling you I know where I put it."

"Okay. Tell me what happened when you got here."

He shrugged. "I don't know what I can add. She didn't answer the door, I heard the dog, and I broke the window."

"We'd better call the police."

But I was suddenly hit with a very unlawyerly urge—a need almost. A criminal impulse welling up from the subconscious. Well, not criminal exactly, just unprofessional. A little illegal, too, actually. A very, very naughty idea. I wanted to get a good look at the crime scene before the police did.

It was entirely possible. A rare opportunity to gather information that might help my client's case had been given to me. There were only two problems. One was a hysterical, yipping, nipping little dog; the other was Ricky. How could I do it without involving him?

The answer was that I couldn't. Even assuming I could get in the window without being boosted—even get in the house without letting him know what I was doing—I needed him to quiet the dog.

"Ricky," I said, "did you try the door?"

He looked bewildered. "Try the door?" Clearly the man was a law-abiding citizen at least some of the time—or so he wanted me to believe. Such people did not try to break into houses except when a murdered loved one lay in plain sight.

"When she didn't answer."

"No."

I got up and tried it. It opened. From the doorway you could see that in the living room, a porcelain bowl and a small sculpture had been knocked off the coffee table. I said to Ricky, "We can phone from here. Let Mellors out, why don't you? He must be dying to go outside."

"He already went on the rug."

"He might want to go again."

Obediently Ricky went to get the dog, never guessing that his lawyer was leading him a bit astray, but I thought this might fly with Jacobson and Tillman. I might take a small unauthorized tour of the house before I phoned, but there would be no need to mention that part.

I took off my shoes and jumped up on Katy's sumptuously covered sofa, where I hoped Mellors couldn't reach. But in a minute Ricky came through with the dog in his arms, crooning to him. "He's friendly as a puppy now. I guess I looked like a bad guy, coming through the window."

I wandered through the house, to Katy's office-library. A few things were in disarray, knocked down, knocked aside, like the objects on the floor in the living room. Some were small objects. One was a chair. A couple of pictures hung awry. I tried to imagine how it could have happened. Her killer had chased her, perhaps, and one or the other of them had banged into furniture.

That fit for some things, but not for the coffee table. It was as if he had pushed her, and she had hit it.

The idea brought up a series of very nasty mental pictures—of her tormentor holding her, perhaps by a wrist, walking her through the house to the study, slapping her around as they went.

It was about the pearl. It had to be. I could hear him:

"Where is it?"

Pop, as he slaps her.

She doesn't answer, falls backward, knocking over a chair.

He hits her again and she slams against a wall, knocking pictures off balance.

But why? If Ricky was telling the truth, the pearl was hers—no one else's—and was locally famous. That meant she hadn't stolen it from an irate former owner, and it meant anyone might have tried to steal it from her at any time. Why now? Because they hadn't found it in Sadie's house or office?

Her office stank of various odors I don't want to describe, or even remember. I saw now that there were bruises all over Katy—on her arms, on her face, everywhere I could see. She had been strangled with a curtain tie that was still wound round her neck, and her hands were tied behind her with another. There was disorder here, too, a lot of books on the floor, as if her assailant had banged her against the bookcases time and again. I thought the coroner would find more bruises under her blouse and slacks.

If she had let this happen to protect Ricky, she must have loved him.

The phone was off the hook, on the floor. But my illicit desire to examine the crime scene had dissipated. I'd find another phone. Protecting fingerprints with the tail of my T-shirt, I replaced the receiver and beat it to the kitchen, where there was a wall phone like Marty had.

I called the Monterey cops, asked for Jacobson just for form's sake, and was stunned when she came on the line.

"I didn't think you'd still be there."

"We work on a homicide till it's solved." She sighed wearily and a little smugly. "Weekends, nights, whatever. What can I do for you, Miss Schwartz?"

Quickly I ran down the situation. Jacobson was beside herself. "You did right to call us. Technically it's the sheriff's case, being in Pebble Beach, but we know you, so we'll come along to smooth things along."

I had to admire her euphemism: "Smooth things along" clearly meant horn in on the sheriff's case.

Who cared? For once, I was in the good graces of an officer of the law. It probably wouldn't last, but I'd enjoy it while I could—and hope it helped my client.

Jacobson said she'd notify the sheriff's office, so my only other chore was to call Ava and tell her everything was okay, she wouldn't have to send police. She was avid. I was brusque. I'd probably pay for it.

Outside, Ricky was sitting on the bench, looking bushed, and Mellors was curled up at his feet as if nothing had happened.

"Okay, Ricky, get ready for bad stuff."

"Oh, man. The worst has got to be over. Seeing her like that . . ."

"A couple of things. Where's Amber?"

"Home with a babysitter. Grounded. On account of that little bit of thievery." His inflection was bitter, as if Amber were the cause of his problems.

''They may keep you a long time, and they may even arrest you. You need to know that.''

He nodded.

''You're going to tell them the truth exactly as you told me—don't worry, I'll be there with you the whole time—but you're going to leave out two things. The reason Katy asked you over tonight, and any mention of the pearl. Any mention at all. Tomorrow is soon enough to tell them.''

''Why?''

Jesus, I thought, sometimes the wrong people get to be parents. But I knew that was just my own worry and guilt over my conflict.

''Because I don't want the cops talking to Amber tonight—going to your house and saying, 'We're holding your father in a murder and we want to question you about a missing pearl.' ''

He turned pale, and I was sorry for my nasty thought of a moment before. ''Omigod.''

''Things will be better for her tomorrow. I promise.''

''Why? What makes you think so?''

''Trust me on this, Ricky. I can make it better. But one thing—do me a favor and don't tell anyone I advised you to withhold information, okay? It's not really cricket.''

He nodded, looking as if he hadn't the least idea which end was up. I didn't blame him. If he was innocent, it had certainly been a perplexing hour or so, and it was about to get worse.

CHAPTER 11

It did get worse, but not as bad as it could have gotten. Ricky fell apart and cried and howled about the lost woman he loved and generally came off as such a baby no one in his right mind could have suspected him of murder.

But of course, that's not how cops and sheriffs think. They didn't arrest him only because they didn't have anything on him. They placed the time of death as earlier that day, about the time Ricky was with Julio and me, and he had other alibis for just before and after that would have to be checked. They didn't have a witness, and they didn't have fingerprints or other physical evidence. And, not knowing about the pearl, they didn't have a suggestion of a motive beyond the usual lover's quarrel. Actually, that had a lot of merit for them—if they found out there were other men in her life, and they almost certainly would if Ricky's suspicions were correct, that wouldn't look good for our team.

But the point is that they had no reason to arrest him that night. We were out of there by ten, and I had miles to go before I slept. I had to get to my other client—the one who was still on the loose—and talk some sense into her.

I heard the gentle buzz of the television as Julio opened the door, and then there he was, in black sweats. Black sweats with nothing underneath them. I felt small beads of moisture form on my forehead, and hoped he couldn't see them.

I said: "I thought Esperanza didn't watch TV."

"Rebecca."

"I'm sorry to drop by so late."

"Come in. You left so suddenly."

Esperanza was lying on the floor in the living room, covered with a blanket, eyes at half-mast, but fixed doggedly on the TV.

"She's allowed two hours on Saturday night," Julio said, "and she gets to watch cartoons on weekends."

I sat down on the floor and kissed her cheek. "Hi, client. We have to talk."

"Hi. Why'd you leave so quickly?"

"Come in the bedroom and I'll tell you."

Julio said, "Wait a minute—how about me?"

"Sorry," I said. "This is privileged."

Once we were in Esperanza's room, I spoke with no preamble. "Honey, we have to tell your dad. Tonight. To stop something bad from happening."

"How bad?"

I knew where that could lead—"pretty bad"; "Really, really bad?"—so I headed it off: "Now, don't faint, okay? Can you handle this? Amber might be in trouble."

"I'm not going to faint." She sounded slightly annoyed, as if I'd been talking down to her—as if she wasn't the sort to faint at the mere mention of Amber, and didn't see why I didn't understand that. Her dip in the bay had changed her, I thought.

"Somebody else got killed, honey."

Her lip quivered as she tried to get up the courage to speak.

"I don't think it's anybody you know. A woman named Katy Montebello."

"Ricky's—" Her eyes were huge with surprise, but she stopped herself in midblurt.

"Ricky's what?"

She spoke with dignity: "Amber calls her Ricky's Sugar Mama. Ricky didn't kill her, did he?"

"Of course not. He's my client, too—none of my clients are guilty." I waited for the expected smile. "But she was murdered. And the pearl could have had something to do with it. The police questioned Ricky about it tonight, and I did something I'm not supposed to do—I told him not to tell them he had the pearl. Do you know why I did that?"

She nodded gravely. "Because he would have had to say Amber stole it. Because that's what he thinks. Oh, Rebecca, she's so brave! She must know I took it—I told Libby, and Libby can't keep a secret. She must have told Amber. Anyway, anybody could figure it out. And Amber never told Ricky. I feel so awful."

"Sweetheart, we all get scared sometimes. You did what you had to." Poor kid. With Sister Teresa's hell-and-jail hanging over her, who could blame her?

She took my hand. "Let's go tell Daddy."

Frankly, I was astonished. This was a different child from the quivering lump of protoplasm Julio had had on his hands before the sail.

"Daddy, I have something to tell you."

"I think it's about time, don't you?"

"Promise you won't get mad."

"I promise I won't feed you to Cecil—is that good enough?"

"Oh, Daddy, I've been so bad!"

She ran to him, leaped into his lap, and cried for about twenty minutes before she could talk. So much for the new, adult Esperanza. I guess growing up is a matter of fits and starts.

Julio listened to his daughter's guilty plea with all the gravity of a three-judge panel, made appropriate fatherly noises (but forbore to feed the kid to the wolf eel), and, frankly, didn't seem all that upset that his little darling was a thief. I guess after nearly losing her, it seemed rather a small matter.

He did have some good questions, though—some I should have asked myself. "Who knew you gave Sadie the pearl, *Nena*?"

"Libby."

"Who else?"

"Nobody, I guess."

"Was there anyone near her office while you were talking with her?"

She shook her head. "The door was closed."

"Let me ask you something else. Did you tell Sadie where you really got the pearl?"

Her eyes widened at the idea of letting her idol know she'd stolen something. "No!"

"You told her you found it on the beach?"

She nodded vigorously.

"What did she say when you told her that?"

"Say?" She squinched up her face, puzzled.

"Do you think she believed you? Did she say anything to make you think she suspected something?"

Puzzlement yielded to wonder. She snapped her fingers. And then she burst into tears again.

"*Nena*, what is it?"

"Oh, Daddy, I'm so embarrassed. She knew. She knew! Oh, Daddy, oh, Daddy, Sadie died thinking I was a thief!"

Julio held her and rocked her back and forth. "Honey, she loved you—don't you ever forget that—just like I do. She didn't care what you did. She loved you anyway; do you believe that?"

Esperanza saw the wisdom of that and, in a few minutes, calmed down.

Julio said, "How did you know Sadie knew how you got it?"

"Because she said, 'Are you sure you found it on the beach? Are you really, really sure?' But I just kept saying, 'I did.' *Maybe* she believed me. She might have, don't you think, Daddy?''

When everything had been hashed over and then rehashed, it was agreed it was too late to call Ricky, and that Esperanza would do it first thing in the morning. She tried to get Julio to do it, but he held firm. She didn't have to go to jail, but she did have to say she was sorry.

She kissed us both good night and scampered off to sleep, once again, the sleep of the innocent. I got up to leave, but Julio stopped me. "Have a glass of wine with me."

Wine? After a nightmare on the bay, a close-up of a corpse, several hours in a police station, and a ten-year-old's trauma? A glass of wine with Julio? Surely life could hold no sweeter pleasure. "It's late," I said. "I'd better go."

"Please. I need to talk to you."

"Oh. Well, of course then." Dear, kind Rebecca—always there when you need her. "Could I make a phone call first?"

It was late to call a judge, but worth a try. A boy answered, a teenager. Music blared in the background. Girls shrieked. Conversation hummed.

"Judge Reyes, please."

"Who?"

"Judge Reyes."

"Just a minute." And then shouting, "Hey, Charlie, is your dad a judge?"

Another boy came to the phone. "Can I take a message? My mom's gone for the weekend."

So much for Judge Serita Reyes. Maybe Bruce Parton knew someone else.

Julio's house was so small the kitchen opened off the living room and shared a common counter with it, making it possible to watch him open the wine. Meaning I got to stare without seeming to, contemplating the shoulders of my host. Wondering if it was wise to drink with him.

The wine he chose was a chewy red one, just what I was in the mood for. If he'd brought in something wimpy and white, I'd have probably drunk the whole bottle, trying to find some substance. White's okay for small talk around the pool; you need red for bloodshed.

When we were settled decorously at opposite ends of the couch, Julio said, "Rebecca, Sadie may have been killed for that thing."

Didn't I know it.

"You know what? I might be the last person to have seen her alive. She called me up on the roof Friday night to talk about Esperanza. That's how I knew she didn't believe the found-it-on-the-beach story."

"Wait a minute. You mean you knew about the pearl all along?"

"No, of course not. When Esperanza swears someone to secrecy, she swears half a dozen people, I guess."

"Weaving her tangled web."

He nodded. "Actually, I shouldn't say she called me up to the roof. That sounds imperious, and Sadie wasn't like that at all. I popped into her office for something and she asked me if I'd like to go up with her. She was in invertebrates, you know, and there's a research lab up there, where they were doing experiments with urchin eggs. She wanted to take a look, she said, and thought I might like to join her for a little break."

"Odd." Unless it was a come-on. What else could it be?

But Julio shook his head. "Not odd at all. Sadie had allies and she had enemies. Mostly allies, to tell you the truth, but—I hate to say it, but there was Marty, for one. You've seen what that third floor is like; even though she was the only one who could close the door, she never was comfortable discussing private things in her office. She'd start whispering, and you wouldn't be able to communicate. So she got in the habit of going up to the roof, especially around six or six-thirty—did most of her hiring and firing up there. She loved it up there after work—said she could think better. I have to admit she knew what she was doing—it was the perfect place for a private discussion.''

"Romantic." I was jealous.

"Very. Anyway, she got me up there and she said something very strange had happened. She said Esperanza had been by, and she was worried about her and said she thought Esperanza needed help. Needed to go to a therapist, I mean.''

"Isn't that a little pushy for an employer? I mean, it's your private business.''

He looked confused. "No. I mean, Sadie and I talked about Esperanza all the time; she helped me a lot.''

I remembered how he'd enlisted my aid as well.

"And of course, something *was* bothering Esperanza. The divorce. She was still drawing pictures of herself and Sylvia and me—she is still. Did you know children of divorced parents do that for a long time?''

I shook my head.

"She'd told Sadie," he continued, "that she felt guilty about it—that she was afraid she was the one who caused it. And Sadie said that night that she wasn't getting better, she was reaching some kind of crisis. Because she'd done something to draw attention to herself, she said. She said it was a cry for help.

"I asked what, of course. But she said she couldn't tell me, that would be violating Esperanza's confidence. But that she'd done something out of character, and she wanted adults to know about it, and that I ought to listen to her. But I said I couldn't listen to her when she hadn't told me anything. . . .'' He paused. "Well, anyway, we got into an argument. It was so damned frustrating, her not telling me what was going on. Now I see what it was. It was about the pearl. She knew Esperanza hadn't found it on any beach.''

"Did anyone see you go up with her?''

"Sure. Lots of people were working late."

"It's odd no one mentioned it to the police—I mean, that they haven't talked to you about it."

"Oh, they have. Don't worry, they have."

And they still thought Marty a better suspect.

"So how did you and Sadie leave it? Were you still angry with each other?"

"No. Thank God. Wouldn't that be a terrible thing to live with—that your friend died angry with you? Finally she convinced me. I saw it wouldn't be fair to Esperanza to tell what she knew. In the end we kissed and made up."

Damn. I was jealous again. "Did you leave together?"

He spread his hands. "I left her there. She still hadn't looked at the urchin eggs."

We were silent. "I saw Marty on the way out," he said finally. "She was leaving, too."

For her date, I supposed, but I wondered why Julio mentioned her. He poured more wine, which I drank gratefully.

He said, "Then I came home and tried to talk to Esperanza about her problems, but that was pretty hard, considering I was more or less in the dark as to why I was doing it."

I said, "She's a lovely child."

And Julio said, "Could we talk about something besides Esperanza for a while? Sometimes I forget I have any identity besides 'Daddy.' "

"It must be hard being a single father."

He shook his head. "I mean it. Something else, Rebecca. Like why a smart, successful woman drives a crummy old Volvo."

I was insulted. "You don't like my car?"

"It's just not you. You need a—"

I wasn't about to let him finish. Who cared what he thought I needed? "You know what I hate about this state, and this decade, and this point in history? Materialism turned into a virtue. The only thing in hell wrong with my car is it's not fashionable. What kind of culture is this where expensive things like cars are throwaway items, subject to the whims and caprices of fashion?''

Julio laughed long and hard, as if he rather enjoyed a good delivery on a midnight rant.

The wine had done its work. We killed the bottle, and when I got up to go, I felt infinitely better than I had when I arrived. Friendly was one of the ways I felt. I wondered briefly if Julio would make a pass, but I was sure he wouldn't. We didn't have that kind of relationship. I threw my arms around him, meaning to kiss him on the cheek, and came to consciousness about half a century later, swimming up slowly, surprised to find that my eyes were closed, that I was still standing, that there was more in the room than Julio's mouth.

He'd moved so fast, I hadn't even noticed, just found myself engulfed. In lips. In passion like I remembered from a long time before, but had almost forgotten about.

CHAPTER 12

"Get out of here! This is not your home, get out!"

"This *is* my home, goddammit! I paid for it so you could pursue that hobby you call a career."

"Hobby! For your precious Sadie, it was a religious vocation, for me it's a hobby, you fucking hypocrite!"

The female voice was Marty's, and the male one Don's. I glanced quickly at my bedside clock—almost nine-fifteen, which didn't surprise me. I'd been up past one the night before. What did surprise me was the presence of either half of this morning comedy team, especially Marty. Don must have arrived home from his business trip. But why the hell had the police let Marty out? Had they arrested someone else? Someone they suspected of having killed Katy Montebello as well as Sadie?

I rubbed my eyes, thinking to throw on clothes, race downstairs, and demand to know what was going on. But then it occurred to me that wouldn't be tactful. Also that I couldn't bring myself to do it. I was too embarrassed, I told myself. And, more to the point, far too curious.

"Would you shut up? You're going to wake the children."

"I thought you came to get the children."

"I didn't plan to terrify them, however."

"Goddammit, you started this, not me!"

"You're the one who ordered me out of my own goddamn house!"

"A house that you left to go live with your floozy."

I held my breath. There was real potential for violence here.

Instead of the crack of fist on soft flesh that I half expected, there was silence, silence for so long, I was puzzled. And then I came bolt upright as the truth of it hit me: *Omigod, he's choking her!* I threw off the covers and was halfway out the door when I heard a sob, a deep, masculine sob that sounded as if it had been held in far too long.

"Oh, Marty, I can't believe she's dead!"

Marty said, "Oh, Don!" as concerned as if he were a younger Keil with a skinned knee, and I pictured her opening her arms to him.

I thought briefly that it was no wonder that Dr. Freud had been puzzled by women, because so was I, and I was one. The hell of it was I was also thinking that, much as I hated to admit it, I might have done the same thing. But it occurred to me that Marty and I were two very different creatures. I might have put my anger and hurt aside because I'm a sucker for birds with broken wings. (This doesn't mean I'm a suffering angel—I know perfectly well that's probably more about power than compassion, but it's still wimp behavior, and I do it because I can't help it.) Marty, on the other hand, always had an angle. What was it this time?

I got dressed slowly, listening to Don's sobs, now genuinely more embarrassed than curious. I didn't want to be a fly on this particular wall, and I was sure Keil, Libby, and Ava didn't either (well, Keil and Libby anyway).

Finally Marty said, "I'm sorry I called her a floozy."

"You were upset."

"Leave the kids with me, Don. I've just spent two days in jail."

"Leave the kids with you?"

"Please, Don."

"Rebecca's here, isn't she? And your mother? Marty, I'm

all alone. I've just lost Sadie—I need something. I've been flying for two days—"

"Flying! I've been in *jail*!"

"Jail!" I could tell it hadn't sunk in the first time she said it. "For what?"

"For killing your little girlfriend, asshole. As if I cared who you're fucking. As if I weren't *thrilled* to get rid of you."

Don said, "*Did* you kill her?" in an utterly bewildered tone of voice, as if the thought had just occurred to him, and as if he considered it very possible indeed.

"Did I kill her! No, I didn't kill her. I was framed, goddammit. They let me go when they got the autopsy report. She was dead before she was stabbed—stabbed in the eye with my letter opener, by the way. The letter opener you gave me."

"Oooohhh." It was a loud, masculine moan—Don's—but it was followed quickly by a scream of distress from Libby's room.

"Mommy, shut up! Shut up!"

I heard the sound of small racing feet on the stairs. "Daddy, Daddy, Daddy!"

Libby must have catapulted into his arms. I heard restless sounds from Keil's room and knew that his pride wouldn't allow him to do what Libby had done, and felt terribly, terribly sorry for him. And for her. I even wasted a little sympathy on Ava, for having to listen to all that profanity.

The funny thing was, it suddenly occurred to me that Libby had acted more adult than all the rest of us put together. Neither parent should have exposed the kids to so much darkness, so much ugliness, such nasty weeping emotional sores. Ava and I should have stopped it, should have protected them. I was ashamed that I hadn't and determined not to let them get away with starting up again. I found my shoes and put on red lipstick, for authority.

"Hello, Don." He and Libby were sitting at the table, Marty making oatmeal, wearing a pair of shorts and a T-shirt, hair clean but dry, a hint that she'd gotten home the night before and washed away the aroma of jail.

Don also must have gotten home the night before; at any rate, he hadn't come here directly from the airport. He was wearing Monterey clothes—faded gray jeans and a turquoise polo shirt, complete with pony. His thin, brownish, nondescript hair was mussed, and his glasses were spotted.

He was not a handsome man at the best of times, though he had a square enough jaw, but right now he was showing the strain of deep loss and draining travel. His shoulders, usually so proudly held in an entrepreneur's almost defiant posture, were slightly hunched. His skin looked gray and crumpled.

"Rebecca. I hope we didn't wake you." He made to stand, but I waved him back down.

"It was time to get up, anyway. Marty, it's good to see you home." (I had to say this because she was my client, but I kept my fingers crossed.)

"Rebecca," said Libby in that singsongy way kids have, making four or five syllables out of three. "Have you got a boyfriend?"

I supposed she was trying to keep the talk on safe ground, any old subject but murder and hate. "I sort of do," I said, pouring myself some coffee. "He's in Cambridge right now, though. In Massachusetts—you know where Boston is? It's near there."

"I mean a new one."

"A new one?"

"Esperanza called this morning. Real early."

I was beginning to get her drift. I said, "I stopped to see her last night. About the white thing." I winked, trying to make contact on another level, a shared secret that Marty and Don couldn't get in on.

But Libby wouldn't be stopped. She said, "Esperanza says she saw you and Julio making out after she was supposed to be in bed."

"We weren't—" I tried to speak, but it did no good. I couldn't be heard above Marty.

"Julio!" she shouted. Her back was ramrod-straight with fury. "Julio Soto?"

As if we both knew a thousand Julios.

"Julio!" she shouted again.

So Julio was "J." But what to do? Better not to bring it up in front of Libby and Don.

I said, "Marty, if we have something to discuss, let's discuss it."

"I leave my children in your care and you throw yourself at the father of my daughter's little friend!"

It's funny how people with children, even those who abuse them one way or another, use the kids as weapons of self-righteousness.

Libby gave me a horrified look, unable to believe what she'd started, thoroughly ashamed. This wasn't fair to her. It simply wasn't fair. And I'd come downstairs to protect her.

"Libby, I'm really sorry," I said, meaning sorry I couldn't help her, but of course, she misunderstood.

She rushed to my rescue: "But you didn't do anything. Anybody could see Julio has a crush on you."

To which Marty replied, "Rebecca Schwartz, you *bitch*!"

"I didn't realize," I said, choosing my words carefully, "that I was stepping on your toes."

"Stepping on *my* toes. Do you think I give a good goddamn about that womanizing *Hispanic* person?"

The way she spat it out, she might as well have used the pejorative for Hispanic as the word itself.

"He's been involved with every woman in Monterey *except* me. This is about you, not me, Rebecca. I thought you of all people could be trusted not to get hot pants for some good-looking *chili pepper*."

I heard, not bells this time, but a country song about poker that my southern law partner had taught me. I knew when to hold 'em, I knew when to fold 'em.

"Sweetheart," I said to Libby, "this isn't a good time for houseguests. I have to leave now. I'll call you later."

She nodded, a tear in her eye.

To the company at large, I answered, "If anyone wants me, I'll be at the Pelican Inn." And I was outta there.

Thinking about the restful vacation I'd planned, I wondered briefly if I could get away with simply getting in the Volvo and driving. Driving home to my finny friends in their tiny little watery habitat without a strand of kelp in it.

But I couldn't, of course. I had my clients, Ricky and Esperanza, though not Marty anymore, I supposed, that fiery little chili pepper. The phrase made me laugh now. It wasn't the worst epithet I'd ever heard, but it was the thought that counted, and the thought was revolting. How dare she speak that way in front of Libby?

I was in deep. Whose daughter was Libby anyway, Marty's or mine? Marty's, of course—I wasn't going to kidnap her—but why couldn't people with children treat them any better? And how could Don let Marty get away with that garbage? The wimp.

Well, anyway, I'd found out one thing. Put her in jail a couple of days, confront her with her ex-husband, threaten to steal her boyfriend, and she no longer resembled a cucumber.

There could have been a problem at the Pelican Inn. It was tourist season and I had no reservation. Even if I had, there could have been another problem. Check-in time was hours away.

However, luck was on my side. Someone had phoned me—

someone so insistent I must be there that the clerk had decided the caller was right and earmarked a room for me, one that was already made up—presumably the extra one you suspect every hotel of saving in case the governor drops by.

I found all this out by asking without much hope if they had any vacancies. One clerk raised an eyebrow at another. "Uh-uh," was the answer. "We have to save it for that Rebecca Schwartz person."

An interesting five minutes ensued while things were sorted out, but once I'd found out they were saving a room for me, they could hardly take it back. In another five minutes, I was relaxing on my own pillow, contemplating my unwitting benefactor—Mr. Ricky Flynn, who, I surmised, had phoned Marty's house and been summarily referred.

I was grateful, I was hungry, and I was nostalgic for Sunday morning brunch with Rob. I phoned my client and offered to treat him to a meal. Did Ricky Flynn decline? Not likely.

CHAPTER 13

He knew a lovely place quite near Cannery Row—a coffeehouse sort of place that reminded me of spots in Berkeley, because it had a courtyard, something we Fogville denizens consider a rare treat. They offered the obligatory champagne-for-Sunday that Rob maintained had been invented for the ease and comfort of afternoon delighters, but which I'm quite sure is intended to ensure women a sound snooze while their men are engrossed in television sporting events. I felt a need to keep a clear head, so there was twice as much for Ricky.

Today he was wearing jeans, running shoes, a Hussong's T-shirt, and his baseball cap. I got the impression this was his habitual fashion statement. It suited him.

"Esperanza called this morning."

I nodded, trying not to look smug. "I thought she would."

"In fact, Amber's over at her house now. Boy, am I going to have to work hard to make it up to the kid—grounding her and all that for no reason. I really feel bad about not believing her."

He was sounding oddly like a father and a grownup. I almost didn't recognize him. "She did a pretty amazing thing, I thought. Taking the heat to protect her friend."

And I was a little worried about that kind of self-sacrifice, but I was probably being a yenta. It was straight out of childhood fantasies. If Amber and Esperanza were anything like me and my little friend Maya, they'd probably sworn blood oaths with lipstick to be best friends forever and ever, and always, always come to the other one's rescue, and never, never let the other one down. Of course, when Maya and I had become blood sisters, I'd imagined the trouble would come from evil magicians who might hold one of us captive in a stone castle, but I suppose that's just a metaphor for your dad saying you're grounded.

"She's a stand-up kid," Ricky said. "I'm really proud of her." He carefully selected a corner of his omelet, cut it, chewed, and swallowed before he said, "I haven't called the police yet."

"You can let them know about the pearl as soon as we're done here. But do me a favor—promise you don't wait any longer than that." I looked at my watch. "In fact, promise to do it by three o'clock. No later. I'll call Jacobson and tell her to expect your call."

"Okay." He masticated some more. "Jeez. I feel terrible about Esperanza. I mean about her trying to kill herself."

So that was why he'd called. He wanted me to tell him it was all okay. I sighed. Esperanza felt guilty about Sadie, and now Ricky felt guilty about Esperanza. The Sheffield Pearl had left a trail of carnage and guilt. I was beginning to think it had a curse on it.

Well, anyhow, I could help Ricky out—that is, if he wanted some Sunday morning amateur psychologizing. I'd thought more about Esperanza and I was dying to get my theories on the table. "The pearl was just a trigger," I said. "Or rather, Sadie's death was. I think the kid's depressed about her parents' divorce. Julio tells me she still draws pictures of the whole family all together."

"Jeez," he said again. "Amber stopped doing that a long time ago."

"Esperanza's just going to have to work through it. Maybe Julio will send her to a therapist or—who knows?—maybe that plunge in cold water will have a reviving effect."

For good luck I didn't say it aloud, but I thought it already had. I'd felt it in her body language, in that way I could tell she'd made a decision for living.

Ricky looked at me like I was nuts.

Who needed it? I changed the subject.

"Ricky, I need to know some things."

I watched his face for flickers of fear or guilt, but a waitress stepped between us, pouring champagne.

When he had drained half his newly filled glass, he said, "You're the lawyer," and collapsed laughing. I didn't know if it was strong drink or if he was always a dim bulb. Probably, as Marty had suggested, effect followed cause.

"We really need to talk about yesterday."

"About Katy—finding Katy's body?"

I shook my head. "About what you were doing in the warehouse yesterday morning."

"What warehouse?" He shoveled in a mouthful of hash browns.

"The old Hovden warehouse. The one the aquarium uses for office space. I'll spell it out: where Marty's and Sadie's offices are. The third floor."

He made a face, picked up a bottle of ketchup, gave it a few whacks, and drowned the remaining hash browns. "Yesterday morning? Saturday?"

"Uh-huh. You were running away. I was chasing you. We met at Julio's about an hour later."

He stared at me, chewing with his mouth open, revealing things a doctor shouldn't have to know about, let alone a lawyer. But I was damned if I'd avert my eyes.

Finally he swallowed and wiped his mouth as daintily as if he hadn't just showed me a scene out of Fellini's *Satyricon*. "Could you run that by me again?"

"Ricky, I saw you. We were both there. I chased you all the way down the stairs. Don't play dumb with your lawyer."

I paused, hoping I sounded like his most feared school-teacher. "What the hell were you doing there?"

"I don't know."

"You don't know?"

"If I was there, I must have been walking in my sleep."

"Running in your sleep."

"Rebecca, can I ask you something? Do you do drugs? Because if I've got a lawyer who does drugs, I gotta rethink this."

"Oh, shut up."

"I was at a job yesterday morning. Working on some-body's addition in Pacific Grove. Remember what I told the cops? Did you think I was lying about that?"

I did remember. It was easily checked. But couldn't he have left and then returned? I didn't want to think about it. If he could have left to go through Sadie's desk, or whatever he'd been doing at the warehouse, he could have left to kill Katy.

I said, "I hope your alibi is as ironclad as you think it is."

"Me, too. If my own lawyer doesn't believe me . . . Jeez." He inhaled a little more champagne.

"It's not that I don't believe you, it's just that there are a few pieces of the puzzle we haven't talked about."

"There's *more*?" His tone said he was sick and tired of answering these dumb grown-up questions and couldn't wait to get back outside to his little friends.

"Quite a bit."

The waitress reappeared. "More coffee?"

"Please." I wanted to make the point that we were going to be here awhile.

I added cream and no-cal sweetener, a contradiction, but who cared? Stirring slowly, I said, "What kind of terms did you and Sadie part on?"

"Sadie and me? Huh?" His voice rose; his brows drew together in fury.

I nodded.

"You mean, did the mighty Ms. Swedlow grace my humble abode that day and say, 'Rick, I think I'll get murdered this afternoon and I wanted to make sure I checked it out with you first'?"

I was sick of his kids' games. "I mean, when the two of you broke up."

"Broke up? What do you mean broke up?" He sounded so taken aback, I knew I'd made a mistake.

"You didn't break up then. You were still seeing each other."

"Seeing each other? You mean romantically?"

I nodded.

"I don't get this. First you tell me I'm where I'm not, and then you tell me Sadie was my girlfriend."

"She wasn't?"

"No. Read my lips: Uh-uh. Never. Not even a little bit. No way, Jose."

I leaned back, exhaling. "I guess I was misinformed."

"Someone *told* you that?" He was starting to get red in the face, either from the champagne, the sun, or high emotion.

I didn't say anything.

He whispered, "Marty." And then he practically yelled, "That *bitch*!"

People turned to stare, and he dropped his voice. "*Marty* and I were involved. Not Sadie and me. Not that I wouldn't have loved to. But Sadie wasn't like that."

"Wasn't like what? Didn't sleep around?"

"Didn't even flirt. All business. But in a nice way." He got that look men get when they're talking about a woman they've admired but couldn't get—kind of like brown-robed saints in religious paintings, staring up at the sky, at angels, or maybe at Lucy-with-diamonds. To be perfectly frank, it's a look of utter idiocy.

"Tell me about you and Marty," I said.

"She hit on me at a party, after we got that last exhibit up. Amber was at her mom's, so why not?"

"When was it?"

"I don't know. Eight or ten months."

"Can you get any closer? It's important." (Well, maybe not important, but it would sure provide some insight into Marty's marriage.)

"I remember now. It was at Christmas—I was feeling sorry for myself."

"Before Sadie came here?"

"Oh, sure."

"So Marty went out on Don." I shouldn't have said it aloud.

"With anything in pants."

"What?"

"Hubby traveled a lot."

"I wonder how he met Sadie."

"Party at *their* house. Marty was always throwing them— I guess she thought it was the corporate thing to do. I watched it happen. Marty was so busy chasing Julio, she didn't even notice they sat down on the floor by the hearth and stayed there for an hour and a half."

That I could believe. I said, "How long did you and Marty keep seeing each other?"

"Month or two, I guess. It kind of petered out. Just one of those things."

"Can you think of any reason she'd say you and Sadie were involved?"

"Oh, she thought so. I guess she and I ran out of gas about the time Sadie got here. So then when Sadie'd been here a couple of months, and she saw how much competition she was, she, like, started calling me again." He pulled his hat down against the sun. "I wasn't interested, you know what I mean? I guess I was in love with Katy. I didn't want to see her anymore. So she accused me of porking Sadie. She had this *thing* against Sadie.''

"Well, Sadie did shoplift her husband in her own house."

"Sadie, hell. That dude was *ready*, you know that?"

"Want some more coffee?"

He swiveled his neck for the waitress. "Wouldn't mind another drop of champagne."

"I'm going to the ladies'."

I felt as if I'd been the one drinking to excess. This brunch was beginning to feel like time spent in the Twilight Zone. Ricky seemed to be taking each of my assumptions and systematically destroying them. Could I believe him?

On some things, probably. But which ones?

I'd have to sort that out later. For now, what was left? Ah, yes, I remembered. His changed status at the aquarium.

Returning refreshed and relipsticked, I said, "Could we talk about something that could help your case?"

"What case? I thought I was off the hook."

"I hope you are. But I thought of something that might help if Tillman and Jacobson start sniffing around again."

"Which one's which? Is Jacobson the woman?" He was starting to slur.

"Yes. Sergeant Paula."

"She's kind of good-looking."

I lifted an eyebrow, which prompted a slightly unwelcome knee-pat: "Course, you are, too."

"Tell me, Ricky, who were you hitting on at Marty's party? With Marty and Sadie busy?"

"God, I can't remember. . . . " He looked as if he were genuinely trying to.

I took pity on him. "I was just kidding."

"Oh. Guess you think I'm the kind of guy that—"

"Honest, I don't think anything." Anything much. "Listen, two important things."

"Two!"

"Two. Remember when you came over to Julio's yester-day? Before I was your lawyer?"

He nodded.

"You sounded as if you were worried about your job, with Sadie gone."

"That wasn't because Sadie loved me so much. I guess she thought I'm pretty much of a good-for-nothing asshole like everybody does. Listen, I still do my art, you know? Nobody thinks so, and I hardly have time with Amber and all, but I do, goddammit, I do!" His face was decidedly red now, but not from the sun, and not from anger.

I steered him back to the subject. "So if Sadie wasn't your special advocate, why were you worried?"

"Because that goddamn Warren Nowell hates my guts. I just met that bastard a few years ago, but I feel like I've known him my whole life. You know that? This town's like that."

I waited.

"His mother was my fifth grade teacher, can you be-lieve that? The teacher from fuckin' hell. Ran her god-damn classroom like fuckin' Auschwitz. Bitch. Goddamn harpy."

He belched, a faraway look in his eyes—or maybe he was just having trouble focusing.

"You know what she used to do? We had this mother-fuckin' white rat in there, and this little kid named Willie—little Willie Oppenheimer—he was terrified of rats. Couldn't stand to look at the thing. Started to shake whenever it was time for the science lesson and we had to feed the animals—we had some snakes, all kinds of things, they didn't bother Willie. The rat was all that did.

"Well, that bitch of a Nowell, she told him the only way to get over it was to make friends with the thing you're afraid of, and she said a certain day was the day he was going to have to feed the rat, and the poor kid stayed home, but I guess he couldn't stay home forever. So he came back and she made him do it, and he was shakin' and sweatin' and turnin' blue and everything, but she made him do it anyhow.

"He must've moved too fast or something, he was so scared—I don't know exactly what happened, but the rat ran up his shoulder and got loose in the room. Kid was so scared, he peed his pants. So was that enough for Mrs. Adolf Nowell? Not even close. *She didn't let him go home.* Made him sit there the rest of the day with his pants soaking wet. *And* she tried to make him catch the rat, but he got sick."

"You mean threw up?"

"Nah, I think he almost fainted. Had to put his head between his knees and lie down on the floor and everything. Smelling of pee the whole time."

Pretty horrible, but was he ever going to get back to the point?

I said, "So you hold Warren's awful mother against him?"

"Hell no!" His fingers closed into a fist, with which he banged the table. People would have stared again if there'd been any left, but we were living it up in lonely splendor. "Warren's a goddamn wimp. I can't stand a wimp, can you?"

"I thought you said he was the one who hated you."

"He knew about Katy and me."

"I don't understand. Why would he care?"

"Because he was a goddamn wimp! Because he could never get a woman like Katy in a million years."

"What are you getting at, Ricky? He wouldn't need one—he's got a perfectly good wife, and doesn't strike me as the roving-eye type. Frankly, I don't buy jealousy as the reason he hated you."

He laughed, too far gone to get his feelings hurt. "You're a sharp one, you know that? Pretty sharp lawyer I got. Okay, okay, he wasn't jealous. He was a snob. Katy was his mother's best friend—they went to college together or something—that's how Warren got his damn job in the first place. With a little help from 'Aunt Katy.' That's what he called her. He didn't like the help messing with her. It was that simple."

"How would he even know you were seeing her?"

"He saw us at a party once. He saw her looking at me. Katy never was good at hiding her feelings."

Right. I decided to admit what I knew: "Frankly, Ricky, I hear Warren has good reason other than 'Aunt Katy' to be angry with you. I hear you like to bait him."

He looked astonished. "Bait him?"

"That's what I heard."

He rested his chin on his fist. "You mean like calling him fatty and stuff?"

I shrugged, waiting for more.

"Like teasing him about not knowing how to swim? Oh, yeah, he really did get mad that time I introduced him around to all these girls at a party and said what a stud he was. I don't think that's it, though."

"You don't think that's what?"

"Why he hates me. He knows I hate him, that's all. He just knows. By instinct. The dude's gonna fire me, you know that?"

"I hope not. I know you need the work."

"I'm really going to miss Sadie." His eyes were the soft, sincere ones of the very loaded.

As he walked me to my car, I remembered I'd told him to go straight to the police after our brunch. Now I had second thoughts. "Ricky, why don't you go home, have a half-hour nap, get up, drink some more coffee, and then call the police—don't go over there—and tell them about the pearl.''

He adjusted his baseball cap—nervously, I thought. ''Think I'm drunk, huh?''

''I'm just giving you good legal advice. You never want to walk into a police station with alcohol on your breath. Expecially not with a semifantastic story to tell.'' And then something that had been nagging at me came into consciousness. ''That reminds me. The maid you remodeled the cottage for—''

''Yolie. Great old gal.''

''Was she ever there when you were?''

''Sure. She used to serve us drinks. And sometimes snacks.''

''Ricky, think hard. Was she there the night Katy gave you the pearl?''

He frowned, marshaling resources. ''Yeah. Yeah, I'm pretty sure she was. Made us margaritas.''

''Did she see Katy give you the pearl? Or could she have heard the two of you talking about it?''

''I see what you're getting at—can she verify my story?'' I nodded.

He stroked his cheek, as if checking to see whether he'd shaved. ''I don't know about that. It's a thought, you know that? Yolie might have been there.''

''I think I'll drive out to see her this afternoon.''

''She goes away on weekends. To see her family down south somewhere—Santa Maria, I think. She probably doesn't even know Katy's dead yet.''

''Maybe I could call her. What's her full name?''

''I don't know. Yolie's short for Yolanda, I know that. Some Spanish name, I think.'' He shrugged. ''I don't think I ever heard it.''

''Does she get back on Sunday nights?''

''Yeah. Yeah, I've been around Sunday nights when she

was there—even seen her come back. Gets in around seven, seven-thirty. Say, you want me to go?''

"No, it'll be better if I do it. You just go home and give the cops a buzz—after your nap.''

I waited till he'd left and got out of my car—I needed a walk to clear my head.

CHAPTER 14

I walked in Pacific Grove, along the shore, watching pelicans and gulls (western ones, of course), mostly just drinking in the sea air, thinking about the Sheffield Pearl.

Much as I hated to admit it, I thought Esperanza's nightmarish theory had a lot of merit. Sadie might have been killed for the pearl. She must have had it with her when she went to the roof, perhaps planning to show it to Julio.

But maybe it wasn't true. I'd made a promise to Esperanza, and it was time to try to keep it. Both Marty and Ricky seemed to be off the hook, but Esperanza was still my client. That was the way with *pro bono* work—it always took longer than the paying jobs and was usually more difficult. I walked for forty-five minutes, working off my coffee buzz, just as Ricky (I hoped) was sleeping off his champagne one.

Then I consulted a phone book, made a call, and hung up when a man answered; a man with a familiar voice. Don was home.

The listed address was the one for Sadie Swedlow, the love nest where she'd lured Marty's husband and where she entertained her children on weekends. I was sure Marty looked at it that way—as a usurpation of her possessions, of her children as well as her husband.

It was a modest house in Pacific Grove, a one-story frame house, old and charming, but perhaps a little small for a stepfamily of four. If she'd lived, she and Don would probably have moved soon.

Don was tousled, wearing only a pair of khaki shorts I suspected he'd just pulled on. "Oh. Rebecca."

"I guess I woke you up. I'm sorry."

"Not at all. Not at all. Will you come in?" He didn't move aside to permit me, but I'd come there to go in, and good manners weren't going to stop me.

"Thanks," I said. "We need to talk."

He led me into a living room of wicker furniture and plants—Sadie's taste, I was sure. It was an inappropriate room for a house with two children—a little too delicate and breakable, a little too feminine. The furniture would soon have been replaced with sturdier stuff, I thought.

But for the moment it was lovely, as cheerful as a nineteenth-century house in the country. The windows were open, and the breeze had caught a lace curtain. There was no television or stereo anywhere in sight. The walls were even hung with flowered wallpaper, completing the effect. They were decorated with a child's drawings, Libby's, I was sure.

"Are the kids here?"

He gave me a rueful smile. "No. I lost the argument."

He looked sad and vulnerable sitting there barefoot with his chest naked. I felt intrusive.

"I'm really sorry about this morning," he said. "I was upset."

"You have a lot to be upset about. I'm sorry for your loss."

"Thank you." He leaned over, catching his face in his hands, not wanting me to see his expression. "This is very hard for me."

"Don," I said, "I hope you don't think I'm judging you, that I bear you any ill will because Marty's my friend. Things happen. And anyway, I'm beginning to think I didn't really know Marty at all.''

"She can be difficult.'' His eyes were full of pain. "Sadie was so soft—so sunshiny.'' He stopped. "I'm having a hard time with this.''

It seemed cruel to make him go through it alone. I was furious at Marty. "I'm sorry you don't have the children with you. I think they need to mourn Sadie, too, and I have a feeling they don't think they can with Marty around.''

He looked at me as if I'd just pulled him from a burning building. "Yes. You think that, too?''

I nodded. "I think they really miss Sadie a lot.''

"She was so warm—they'd never been around a woman like that.''

I raised an eyebrow. "Oh?'' He certainly was pulling no punches.

"Marty and I got married when she was pregnant with Keil. She told me later—when she wanted me to know how much she hated me—that she'd gotten pregnant on purpose. I was on her list. A goal. Two goals. She wanted to get married, and she wanted to marry someone successful. Also she wanted a kid. Three goals. Though why she wanted that, I don't know. She isn't the maternal type.''

"And she had Libby because, having had a boy, she then had to have a girl. That was the next goal.'' I was surprised to hear what came out of my mouth, and apparently Don was, too; I could see it in his eyes.

I was on a roll and I wasn't going to stop: "Tell me something. Does she often yell the way she was doing this morning?''

"No. I've never seen that before in my life.''

"She's not the type to get mad?''

"She got mad when I left. First time I've ever seen it.''

"I came here because I need to ask you about something, and I also need to ask a favor.''

"Of course, Rebecca." To my amazement, he smiled; perhaps the anticipation of doing a favor had made him comfortable, given him something he knew how to cope with.

"Did you talk with Sadie Friday? Even Thursday?"

"Both days, but only once on Friday. We usually talked several times a day."

"Did she mention a pearl to you? Something Esperanza brought her?"

He shook his head. "I don't know what you mean."

"Esperanza came into possession of something that might be valuable—she said she found it on the beach. This is going to sound strange, but it looked like a pearl the size of a Ping-Pong ball."

He stared.

"But she wasn't sure it was a pearl, and she took it to Sadie for confirmation. Sadie, I think, recognized it as something she'd seen before—she knew it was genuine. But that isn't the point. The point is that it's missing now. It wasn't in Sadie's desk, but there's a chance she brought it home. I'm wondering if you've seen anything like that."

He shook his head, still staring, trying to take it in. "The police didn't mention it."

"To tell you the truth, Esperanza didn't come out with it right away. She was upset about Sadie's death—"

"They were very close."

"She's an awfully sweet child, isn't she?"

"Yes." He looked befuddled, not sure where I was going with that one.

"I told her I'd try to find it for her. I wonder if you'd help me? I mean—" I wasn't quite sure how to put delicately the fact that I wanted to search his house"—I thought we might look for it together."

Slowly intelligence began to seep into his expression, momentarily replacing the grief and pain. "Rebecca, how much is that thing worth?"

"To tell you the truth, I don't know."

"A lot?"

"Honestly, I have no idea."

"Did Esperanza really find it on the beach?"

It was no good. His mind had worked its way up through the mire of his loss. I wasn't going to get away with a story about a sweet kid we had to help. "No. I'll be honest with you, Don. There's a possibility someone killed Sadie for it."

He stood up, jaw tensed. "Let's look."

We tossed the house, starting with Sadie's underwear drawer and jewelry box, working our way through her file cabinet, the toilet tank, the ice trays, the frozen food packages, the sugar bowl, everything we could think of. We searched Sadie's car as well, and even a fake rock in which she and Don hid their door keys.

We didn't find the pearl—which made me feel jumpy on Esperanza's account—but the exertion was good for both of us, I think. Don had more color when I left, and seemed to have recovered some of his energy.

I left thinking I'd never spent so much time with Don, never really known what he was like. I liked him enormously. Anyone missing his girlfriend so desperately had to be a person of strong feelings. And all along I'd thought he was just another cold-blooded businessman.

Marty was the warm one, I'd thought, because of her love of the ocean. That seemed out of character now that I knew the ice-cube Marty. But I knew it wasn't, really. It was the doorway to her good side, the one she didn't seem to know about herself. It would be easy to find it, I thought. If she could just work her way up the Darwinian ladder—transfer her affections from fish to reptiles—it wouldn't be that much of a step up to birds and then on to mammals—rodents first, say, and then on up to the lower primates. From orangutans she could go to gorillas, and next thing you know, she might even get interested in bald-bodied apes.

I was about a block from my hotel and engrossed in this silliness—I often get giddy when I drive—when I noticed Libby trudging along the street with a backpack, loaded down and forlorn.

I waved and honked, but instead of breaking into a delighted grin, she covered her mouth with her hand, terror plain on her guileless features. Confused, she forgot to watch her step and stumbled on a raised piece of sidewalk.

I pulled to the curb, jumped out, and helped her get up. "What is it, honey?"

"I fell down."

"I don't mean that. You looked like you were afraid of me."

"I'm not afraid of you." She sounded mad now, had gone into a classic pout. She started to walk on.

I said, "Why don't you let me give you a lift?"

"No, thanks. I'll be okay."

"Where are you going?"

She looked confused.

"Libby? Is something wrong?"

"No!" She fell into my arms, mouth working as she tried not to cry.

I stroked her hair and assured her it would be okay, the words sounding stupid and dishonest even to me. Sure it would be okay—in about twenty years if she could find a good shrink. Things in this kid's life had gone seriously wrong, and I wasn't going to be able to kiss them away.

Libby let go of me and bent down for her backpack. "I have to go now."

"Are you going to Esperanza's?"

She shook her head.

"Amber's?"

"Uh-uh."

"Your dad's?" But surely not. It was too far to walk.

"I'm just taking a walk." She spoke defiantly, but a nervous toss of the head gave her away.

I thought I understood the backpack, even knew why she just happened to be so close to my hotel. Like Dr. Freud, I don't believe in coincidences. With Sadie gone, Libby needed someone to talk to—maybe unconsciously, but she was looking for me, I thought. Sure. Much the way Julio was probably hanging by the phone waiting for my call.

"Libby," I said, "are you running away?"

She nodded gravely, almost hanging her head, the way kids do when they fear dire punishment.

"I don't blame you," I said.

Her head snapped up, her face unbelieving. "You don't?"

"I'd probably do the same thing in your shoes. Come on. Let's go get some ice cream."

"I'm not allowed to."

"I thought you were running away—aren't you a free agent?"

Her face brightened. "I know! I could have frozen yogurt."

Oh, boy. A real tough cookie, this one. To Marty she was "difficult"; to Ava she was "bad"; and she was so brainwashed, she wouldn't even eat butterfat.

She got chocolate chips on her strawberry yogurt swirled with white chocolate. And then, perhaps regretting the healthful strawberry influence, she decided on Oreo crumbles as well. I had a Diet Coke.

I was curious. "Would you have run away if you'd been at your dad's house today?"

She colored. "I don't think so. At least Daddy'd be home."

"Your mom isn't?"

"She drove Grandma home. I wanted to go; I thought I'd keep her company after she'd been in jail and all—but she wouldn't let me. She just left Keil to boss me." She covered her mouth with her hands and closed her eyes—she'd shoveled in such a big spoonful, her mouth was freezing.

Her mouth still full, she said, "Do you know how much I hate that?"

It was all I could do not to snap, "Don't talk with your mouth full." Chocolate dribbled from the corners.

"How much do you hate it?" I said, absently. I was thinking about Marty's refusal to let the kids stay with Don on a day she declined to spend with them.

"A barrelful."

"How about a truckload?"

"A boatload."

"A planeload."

She looked around before she spoke, mindful that the other customers didn't hear. "A shitload."

"Not so loud. Your grandma will hear."

She had a giggle fit like the ones kids get in *Three Men and a Baby* when the baby wets her diaper. As this is not humor adults can readily share, there was nothing to do but wait till it passed. "You're fun, Rebecca."

"Well, sort of fun. I've got bad news."

"I know. I have to go home." She didn't seem to mind at all.

"Eventually, anyhow. Why don't you call Keil and tell him where you are—and then we'll go to a movie. Want to?"

"Can I have popcorn?"

Born for business, most kids. Always making deals.

When I took her home, finally, I went in with her—or to the threshold, as it turned out—to make sure she didn't get in any hot water.

Marty met us at the door, dressed to go out, California casual in a snug-fitting knit pants outfit. She'd even been at her hair with a curling iron. She wore a squash blossom necklace, and she was preoccupied with fitting matching silver earrings into her ears.

Libby spoke as if nothing had happened. "Hi, Mom. Can Esperanza sleep over?"

"You're grounded tonight, young lady. Keil told me what you did—taking off without even telling him."

"Oh, Mom."

Marty relented a little. "You're going to your dad's tomorrow, but you'll be home Tuesday night. She can sleep over then. How's that?"

"Okay." She smiled as brightly as if her mom had said they were going to Disneyland, and slipped inside. " 'Bye, Rebecca. I had fun."

Marty said, "Thanks for taking care of her. Sorry I can't ask you in—I'm in a hurry."

I wondered if this meant she was no longer angry with me. It wasn't exactly an apology, but maybe that was as close as Marty got to making one.

"Another time," I said.

I'd had to park about halfway up the block from Marty's, on the opposite side of the street. I hadn't yet reached my car when I heard a door slam, heels click. I turned automatically and saw Marty practically flying to her car—apparently she was late. As I got in my car, I saw her pull out. Another car, a dark one, a Chrysler, I thought, pulled out behind her and began to follow at a discreet distance. Or was it my imagination?

It could be, I reasoned, but if it wasn't, I couldn't leave her alone—not with the Monterey murder rate rapidly climbing. I followed the car following Marty.

CHAPTER 15

It was only about seven-thirty, nowhere close to dark, but somehow I never could seem to get close enough to see the Chrysler's license plate. It was a short ride, only as far as a fairly large, fairly impersonal motel where Marty didn't register.

Instead, she pulled into the parking lot, next to a silver compact of some sort, jumped out quickly, and rushed up the stairs, apparently to a room on the second floor. At this point I lost sight of her. I kept a good distance away, because the car that had followed her parked behind hers, perpendicular to it. The driver simply sat there a few moments and then drove off.

I presumed that meant Marty was in no danger, but now I had to know who was in that car—at least I had to get the license number. I stepped on it, finally able to pull up parallel at a stoplight. It was Don in the car.

I leaned over to adjust my radio and busied myself until the car behind me honked, informing me I'd missed the signal. Don was a safe distance ahead. I could only hope he hadn't seen me, but my heart was beating fast.

And that wasn't entirely about my nearly embarrassing almost-encounter. I had to know about that silver compact. I drove back to the motel, took its license number, and found myself heading, without deciding to do so, toward Julio's street.

He had a car like that, his initial was "J," and Marty had yelled at me for going over to his house. So what? How was their romance any of my business?

It wasn't. Anyway, I knew what I knew. I didn't need confirmation.

These arguments did no good. The Volvo seemed to have a mind of its own.

On Julio's block, cars were packed pretty closely together. I drove slowly. Was his car a Nissan or a Honda? Or maybe one of those funny little Fords? And what make was the one at the motel? Why hadn't I noticed?

I only realized I was holding my breath when I released it—I did see a silver compact, though not quite where it was supposed to be. Across the street, in fact. I'd nearly missed it, and had to turn around, craning my neck, to get a good look. It was the right color, but was it really a compact? Was it the same design as Julio's? I slowed down to almost a crawl.

And when I looked back, I saw what was about to happen, too late. I slammed the brake, but didn't stop fast enough. Someone had had the nerve to park, not a normal-sized car, but a recreational vehicle that stuck out far more than the other cars, right in my path. I closed my eyes and braced myself. The thud was hideous. The shock was ugly. I was thrown mercilessly forward. Fortunately, I was wearing my seat belt. My body didn't even bang anything.

My eyes flew open, and I saw that I was awfully close to the beige back end of the RV. My hood seemed to be shorter than it had been a moment before. I sat there, trying to take that in, figure out why that would be, and also trying to catch my breath. If my heart had been beating fast before, it was now doing double time, hammering like John Henry. I could feel it, but I couldn't hear it—because of the shouting.

"Goddammit, you bitch! You stupid goddamn bitch!" I

couldn't see the shouter's face, because his arms were going like windmills.

"Rebecca! Rebecca, is that you?" The second shouter was Julio.

Fear of the first shouter overcame my embarrassment. I jumped out of the car and into Julio's arms, looking for any protection I could get from the mad van owner.

"I just had the goddamn thing painted! Do you see the 'For Sale' sign? Goddamn thing's for *sale*, you stupid bitch!"

Julio said, "Take it easy, Mr. Donahue. What happened, Rebecca?"

"I looked away for a second."

"Mr. Donahue, you really didn't park very well."

I looked at the curb and saw that the van probably was more than the legal eighteen inches away.

"Stupid bitch!" said my persecutor. He was a freckled man of about fifty. His hair had probably once been red, but it was now a pinkish-gray color, what there was of it. The top of his head was a contrasting pink. His suffused face clashed horribly.

On their small front porch was an overweight woman in an apron, which she was clutching and squeezing as if wringing it out. She was probably terrified of the madman she was apparently married to.

I stuck out my hand. "Rebecca Schwartz, Mr. Donahue."

"You wrecked my RV!"

He wouldn't shake.

"Well, I'm sorry about that, but my insurance will pay for it."

"Insurance! I'm supposed to leave on a three-week trip to Europe in a week!"

Maybe he was right—maybe I was stupid. I couldn't really see how that applied.

Julio said, "Rebecca, are you all right?"

I nodded.

"Are you up to moving your car?"

I realized then it was still in the middle of the street. Cars were going around it, but people had come out of their modest homes to inspect the damage. I had become a neighborhood spectacle.

I nodded, and then took a good look at my car. The front end was more or less pleated. I looked back at Julio. "Oh, my God. It's totaled, isn't it?"

He nodded gravely. "You needed a new car anyway."

If I'd expected sympathy for the gaping wound that opened when I saw I'd killed my beloved old Volvo, I'd come to the wrong place entirely. This was the guy who'd complained about my car even when it looked good. Sadness turned to fury, and I would have stalked off if I'd had more than two steps to go. As it was, I gave the door a good slam.

But of course, the damn thing wouldn't start. I had to get the traitor and a couple of other neighbors to help me push it to the curb—after Mr. Donahue consented to move his precious RV—and then I had to endure the humiliation of describing the accident to the teenage policeman summoned by Mr. Donahue:

"But, Miss Schwartz, what were you looking at?"

"Oh, I don't know. I thought I saw a bug."

"A bug?"

"A bee. I thought there was a bee in the car. I tried to swat it."

"I thought you said you didn't know."

"I didn't want to admit it. It's such a stupid thing to do."

"You can say that again," said Mr. Donahue.

"But your windows were closed," the policeman continued.

"Officer, is this really relevant?"

"It just seems so . . . unusual."

Julio offered to take me home, though he seemed to take it for granted I had to be medicated before I could travel.

Without asking, he poured me a glass of wine and one for himself. He sat down and apparently felt I should sit next to him.

"Were you coming to visit, I hope?" he said.

"You didn't go for the bee story?"

"If you weren't coming to visit, perhaps you were watching my house. Don't you trust me, Rebecca?"

He was wearing khaki pants and a black polo shirt, as if dressed for a date. That and the memory of the kiss threw me off for a moment.

And then I remembered about the murders. I was so horrified, I gasped. "You mean was I hoping to catch you on your way to commit another murder, thereby clearing both my clients?"

"Well, I heard that joke about the white rats. I haven't been around that many lawyers, but people say they'll do anything."

That made me mad. "You probably also think Jewish women don't date outside their faith."

His eyes went all twinkly on me. "Esperanza tells me otherwise."

"Little big mouth. Where is she anyway?"

"At Amber's. Could I ask you something?"

Would I go out with him? Sure.

Would I run away with him? Why not?

Would I marry him? Maybe.

"Would you tell me what you were up to when you demolished poor Mr. Donahue's RV?"

I'd had a glass of wine by now, and nothing to eat. I said, "I was trying to see if the silver car across the street was yours."

"I don't understand."

"It's complicated. Maybe I'd better ask you a question."

"Shoot."

"Are you seeing Marty?"

"Seeing her? You mean dating?"

"Something like that. To be euphemistic about it."

His brows knit in confusion. "Marty? Of course not. Why on earth would you think that?"

I thought about whether I had a right to give Marty's secrets away and decided it wasn't the lawyer she'd asked to get the calendar, it was the friend. "Because Marty met someone at a motel a while ago whose initial is J."

Utter disbelief played over his features. Was he talking to a female filbert?

I said, "Oh, hell," and laid the whole thing out for him, from the calendar to Don.

He was still mixed-up. "But what did you care?" he said. "What does it matter who she was seeing?"

"You're making this awfully difficult for me."

"Oh. You were checking on me."

I nodded, knowing I must be the color of Mr. Donahue's scalp.

"Well, that was sweet of you."

"You're handsome, Julio, but I don't know if you're worth losing a car over."

"It was meant to be. That car was no good for you."

"I loved that car." The wound opened up again. I guess I looked as sad as I felt. Julio must have wanted to give me something. Or maybe he was just antsy around the "l" word.

He said: "Everyone knows who she's seeing, by the way. I don't know who she thinks she's fooling."

"Marty? You know who Marty's seeing?"

"Jim Lambert, the chairman of the board."

"Of the aquarium?"

He nodded. "Of course. Haven't you figured that out about Marty? She likes to play the angles."

"I think I'm starting to catch on. Is Lambert married, by any chance?"

"Sure. Why do you think they had to meet in a motel?"

"I get it. So if she covered for him to the point of going to jail, she might have quite an edge with him."

"I happen to know she wants the job Warren thinks he's got."

"Oh, right. She sure does. And she seems to be seeing Lambert every night."

"She probably even pays the motel bills." He was smiling in that way that made me want to look at his mouth until the sun came up. But this was no time for distractions.

"Wait a minute. She acts so wronged about Don's leaving her. Was she going out with Lambert first?"

"You catch on slow, but at least you catch on. To tell you the truth, Marty's kind of a legend at the aquarium."

"You mean—um—" I was trying to think how to put it.

"She screws anything in pants."

I gasped, remembering how mad she'd gotten when I mentioned Julio's name.

"Everything except me and a few others who can outrun her. Poor Ricky got caught, though."

"But—this is what she said about Sadie."

He raised an eloquent eyebrow. Were you born yesterday? it asked. He said, "Are you hungry, by any chance?"

"Starved." But then I remembered what I'd intended to do. "Damn! I was going to go up and see Katy's maid."

"I'll take you."

"You look like you're going somewhere."

"Esperanza and I were going to a movie, but she deserted when Amber called."

I wondered if he knew how attractive the vulnerable routine was, or if he just did it naturally. "Let me buy you dinner," I said. "Something simple—pizza maybe."

Julio made a face. "Ewww. Gross."

"What's wrong with pizza?"

"It's all ten-year-olds ever eat—especially melancholy ones who've just jumped in the bay. I'm going to turn into a pepperoni before Esperanza reaches puberty. Let's get some tempura—she hates Japanese.''

There was something kind of wonderful about sneaking around when the kid was gone. Turning tempura into forbidden fruit made it taste twice as good, the way certain things had tasted in childhood. Pizza probably.

After we'd satisfied our lust for adult fare, we drove out to Carmel, to Katy's wonderful beachfront house with its little servant's cottage. I felt a little weird about this—if Yolanda didn't yet know Katy was dead, I certainly didn't want to be the one to break the news, but it was a chance I had to take.

As it happened, I needn't have worried. The whole place was dark as a cave, and there was no car in the driveway. But Julio was determined our trip shouldn't be wasted. He suggested a walk on Katy's lovely beach.

It was foggy and a little spooky. The moon was waxing, nearly full—a gibbous moon, slightly pregnant and looking her most beautiful in diaphanous veils of fog. The night was too chilly for my thin T-shirt. It was necessary for Julio to put an arm around my waist and draw me close to his body for warmth. Hormones I didn't know I had flowed into my bloodstream. Waves crashed. Diana the moon goddess was out for a frolic at my expense.

She let me see light on the water and the passion in Julio's eyes. But Diana wasn't the only one with us—some little worry-demon, a messenger from the mundane world we'd left behind, tapped me on the shoulder and started nagging.

''Rebecca, you don't know anything about this man.''

''Rebecca, you're only a week and a half out of a two-year relationship.''

''Excuse me, Rebecca, but you always get in trouble with vulnerable men. Do you really want to go back to playing mommy?''

Julio said, ''What are you afraid of?'' Words I first heard from fatso Butch Lieberman in the backseat of a Mustang.

I'd only heard them about a thousand times since—why on earth do men think you're afraid of them when it ought to be obvious you merely find them repulsive?

But this time I was afraid. "I don't know," I said, answering the question honestly for the first time in my life. We sat on a rock and I told him about Rob, that being the best story I could come up with on short notice. But it wasn't exactly the whole story.

"Maybe tomorrow," said Julio, and I snuggled against him, feeling safe for the moment, delighted to stop the subject. "Lunch tomorrow."

"Sure."

"And then we'll buy you a car."

Now, that made me really nervous. Talk about rushing into things—I'd been with the Volvo a lot longer than I'd been with Rob.

CHAPTER 16

As soon as I got back to my lonely motel room, I began to have regrets. Was I crazy to choose a night alone in this overpriced dump over an impulsive cuddle with a man I was starting to like very much?

Like very much, hell. How prissy could I get? I wanted to tear his clothes off. I wanted to see his body in candlelight and kiss every inch of it.

But that wasn't the half of it. I could have handled that.

I was starting to fall in love with him. I thought maybe that was what I was afraid of—what with Rob still calling, Marty flipping out at the mention of his name, a tiny little thing like two murders, and the fact that I'd barely known him thirty hours. Was that possible? Only thirty hours? I shuddered, realizing how strongly I felt about the man.

I tossed and turned and kicked at the covers, angry at myself, and angry at fairy tales that never mention love can make you angry.

Just when I thought I'd never get to sleep, the phone woke me up.

"So how's the little mom? The kids were too much for you, were they? Marty said you'd turned tail."

I rubbed my eyes. "Rob?"

"You were expecting Prince Charles?"

"It's seven A.M.; do you care at all?"

"Oh, sorry. I can never get it straight about the time difference."

"Listen, could you call back later?"

"Sure. But listen. Could you get me up-to-date on the case? I know this sounds weird, but I'm doing a story for the *Boston Globe*. There was another murder, huh? Did Marty do it?"

"I'll call you back," I said, slammed down the phone, and then took it off the hook again—I knew Rob; he'd call back.

Why hadn't I ever noticed how inconsiderate he could be? Julio would never be like that.

The worrywart tapped me on the shoulder again: "Rebecca, dear? In a pig's eye."

However, he hadn't been yet, so I fantasized about him while dropping back to sleep. It was a nice quiet revenge that didn't hurt anybody.

Two hours later, after a croissant and coffee, I took a cab out to the airport, rented a car, and drove to Marty's. Libby met me at the door with so many hugs and kisses, it would have been worth the trip even if Marty had thrown me out.

But her mom was all smiles. "Rebecca. I was going to call you. I'm really sorry I got upset—I mean, I *was* upset—that's why I yelled at you."

"I wanted to talk things over with you."

"Coffee?"

"Sure."

She gave me the cup with the whale's tail and we sat at her kitchen table. She was wearing shorts and T-shirt.

"You aren't going to work today?"

"I'm taking a couple of days off—until the board meets again. I think there's a good chance they'll reconsider their decision about Warren, and I thought I'd take it easy—spend some time with my kids—since I'll be going back to a different job.''

"You sound pretty confident."

"I was always the first choice, I'm sure. But my being in jail was a problem." She smiled as if it were the best thing that ever happened to her.

"I don't think it was a problem—it let you manipulate your way into what you wanted."

"What are you talking about?"

"I understand you're seeing Jim Lambert."

"What is this? Don called this morning and accused me of the same thing."

"It's a small town, Marty."

She drew herself up, as if suddenly remembering to feel insulted. "What did you come here for?"

"I wanted to find out why you got so excited when I mentioned Julio's name."

"Rebecca, I wasn't in the best of moods."

"But what set you off about him? Are you seeing him, too?"

"What business is it of yours?"

"I guess I may as well be honest—I'm interested in him myself."

"You bitch!"

"Wait a minute. We've been that route. You don't like the idea of my seeing Julio. Why?"

She frowned, confused. She said, "Good question," back in cucumber mode. She thought a moment. "I guess I keep thinking he'll come around."

I hoped my inward sigh of relief wasn't audible.

I thought I was beginning to see what made her tick emotionally. "Can I ask you another question?"

"Why not?"

"Were you in love with Don?"

She smiled and sipped coffee to cover her discomfort. "I guess not."

"You know, I really thought you were upset that night in San Francisco. Just a little out of touch with your feelings."

"I was upset!" As if to prove it, she showed me eyes brimming with tears. "I really miss him."

I could bet she did—like she'd miss any cherished possession. I thought when she lost her cool was when things went out of control, a docile husband falling for someone else, a boss—a person in a position to do Marty some good—snapping up the same docile but neglected possession. Jail didn't faze her because she could turn it to her advantage.

But there was one thing that theory didn't cover. She had been anything but cool when we discovered Sadie's body. Of course, it must have been a shock seeing her jacket and her letter opener in such grisly circumstances. Or had she been not at all shocked—merely acting a part, having framed herself to divert suspicion?

I realized with a start that I wouldn't put it past her. She wasn't my friend anymore—she was someone very different from the woman I'd thought she was—and the truth was, she pretty much disgusted me. But she was Libby and Keil's mother, and if I was starting to fall for Julio, that was nothing compared to the way I'd lost my heart to Marty's kids. I was going to have to maintain a semblance of friendliness with her.

So I stayed till I'd finished my coffee, and it was hard, listening to her fresh laments about the way Don had wronged her. Somehow, knowing about Ricky, Jim, and all the gang, I wasn't nearly as sympathetic anymore.

There was time before lunch to satisfy my curiosity on something. I looked up "pearls" in the phone book, found only one jeweler listed, and paid a call. The proprietor was a man named Sidney Silversmith, apparently returned to the trade of his ancestors. I told him I represented a San Franciscan interested in buying the Sheffield Pearl and asked if he knew anything about it.

He shook his head. "You'll never get it now. It'll be tied up in probate."

I listened politely to the tale of Katy's murder, agreed the quest was probably hopeless, but said I had to make a report. Did he know how much it was worth?

"I've never actually seen it. If it's a South Seas pearl of gem quality, it could be worth several hundred thousand. Over a million, perhaps. But I've heard it's a clam pearl."

"I think it might be. How can you tell?"

"A clam pearl has wrinkles. And no luster. Worthless. A curiosity only."

"Worthless?"

"Except to your client." He was practically sneering. "Collectors will pay anything. A large blue abalone pearl is about to be auctioned next week—Sotheby's estimates the value at more than three million dollars." He turned up his palms in seeming amazement. "It's rare. The smaller blue ones—even they're worth fifteen, twenty thousand dollars. But the ones that aren't blue—worth nothing. Even though they get as big as the end of your finger."

"I didn't know abalones made pearls."

"Even conchs make pearls. Except they aren't real pearls. They're calcareous concretions, pink with a flame design. And freshwater pearls come from mussels—did you know that? But clam pearls have the distinction of being ugly."

"And worthless?" I said again.

"That depends. The Sheffield Pearl is famous—and it's supposed to be as big as a golf ball. For all I know, there's someone crazy enough to want it and someone else crazy enough to bid against him. Your client, maybe. If someone wants it, it's valuable. That's how people are." He hunched his shoulders, apparently in disgust at human foibles.

* * *

Julio's appetite for adult fare was still raging. For lunch we went to one of those lazy Susan–style sushi bars, this one with a twist. Each sushi tray was a mechanical sea otter in luxurious repose, your California roll or maguro resting comfortably on its synthetic tummy. In case the patrons weren't already splitting their sides, the owners had tied red bows around the necks of some of the otters and decorated others with leis of fresh flowers. It looked like a place expressly designed to convert ten-year-olds to the eating of raw fish, but Julio said Esperanza would pick up a hagfish before she'd venture into the joint.

"I've tried." He sighed. "Believe me, I've tried. At least she'll eat Mexican food, because she's had it all her life. Amber won't even eat that. And Marty's so strict, Libby doesn't dare eat most things. Taking those three to dinner is like trying to find a cure for anorexia."

"And you don't cook, I suppose."

"Of course I cook. Are you a sexist? You should have seen me at the beginning of the summer. I cooked fantastic things—lobster, moo shu pork, chile rellenos, crab cakes. I outdid myself. I was the dad from Dad Heaven—Robert Young and Bill Cosby in one incredibly frustrated package. How many times do you think *you'd* have to hear 'Ewww. Gross,' before you never picked up a pan again?"

"I might be tempted to pan-fry a ten-year-old."

"Oh, I was. I made the mistake of complaining to Marty, but she took it the wrong way."

"Had her own agenda, did she?"

"Invited Esperanza to sleep over, and me to cook with her, for both girls. She was going to show me how a woman— therefore an expert—did it." He stopped there, but I thought he wanted to say more.

"Don't tell me," I said. "She wanted you to sleep over, too."

He said, "I don't see why a man and a woman can't just be friends. Do you?"

I couldn't answer. I had a whole shrimp in my mouth.

Quickly he said, "I didn't mean you and me, of course."

"It's not the worst idea I ever heard."

"We'll see." I could have sworn the corners of his mouth turned up ever so slightly, as if the battle was won and he knew it. "Shall we go buy you a car?"

I nearly choked on my tekka maki.

"You need a really beautiful car. Gorgeous woman like you. Professional woman. Something jazzy. Something people can see coming for miles away. Something that says, 'I'm Rebecca Schwartz and I'm *zooming* at you.'"

Was he kidding? I didn't even wear nail polish. "I don't know if I'm the zooming type."

"Something in a Mercedes?" He headed his silver compact toward a dealership.

My throat was closing. "Julio. I can't."

"What do you mean you can't?" He opened the door, took my hand, and pulled me out, seeming not to notice the resistance I offered.

A salesman hustled up, a dapper black man in a gray suit, smoothing his jacket. "Beautiful day. Gorgeous day for a new Mercedes. Happy to meet you, sir. My name's Parker Fraley."

Julio made introductions.

"Know what they call me 'round here? Black Magic. You prob'ly think it's 'cause I work a silver-tongue spell on folks, don't let 'em out of here without a new Mercedes. It's not that, though, not that at all. It's 'cause I can make anybody smile, you know that?"

My stomach turned over. He was about to tell the one about the lawyers and the lab rats, I could feel it.

Julio said, "I thought maybe a 560 SL."

"Little convertible. Perfect day for it. You know, you just got to be happy on a day like this—middle of August, almost back to school time. Tell you what—we're having a back-to-school sale today. I'm gon' give you a little ol' 560 so cheap, you gon' want two of 'em."

He opened the door of a sleek red convertible. "You're the one buyin', aren't you, Ms. Schwartz? Jus' sit behind the wheel of this little baby and see if you ever want to get in another car again."

"I can't."

Julio said, "What's this, 'I can't'?"

"It's against my—I just can't, that's all."

Julio blushed. The incredibly handsome, self-assured Mr. Julio Soto turned the same color as the car. "Omigod. The Germans. Magic, I'm really sorry. Another day, okay?"

He hustled me back in his car before I figured out what was going on.

"Rebecca, I forgot. I never thought you might have a thing about German cars. I can't believe how stupid I am."

"Julio, stop. It's nothing to do with being Jewish. I don't know how to break it to you, but I'm a liberal."

The fact that he was driving stopped him not for a moment—he turned and stared, as if at my marbles, even now rolling out the window and onto the road. "I don't get it," he said finally.

"I don't want an ostentatious car."

"You don't want—what?" He stopped, sputtering, took a moment, and collected himself. Finally he said, "Rebecca, here is your problem. You are not from Southern California. As I may have mentioned, I grew up in Santa Barbara, a town half the size of Berkeley with Rolls-Royce *and* Jaguar dealerships. And if you didn't grow up in Southern California, you know nothing about cars. Believe them, because it's true. You're not qualified to pick out a car because you don't understand the true purpose of a car, which is not, repeat *not*, to get from one place to another. A car has one purpose and one purpose only.

"The right kind of buses, with a little planning, could be convenient as hell, carpooling— You know what? Even walking. Walking wouldn't be half-bad for most things, but we never walk. We are busily polluting the planet beyond redemption. And why? To impress our friends, that's why. There is no other reason, believe me." He paused, wrinkling his nose. "You may be wondering why I drive this under-sized excuse for a transportation machine. Well, Sylvia got the good car. It's only temporary, I assure you."

He turned into a lot shiny with new BMWs, and that was okay with me. If he wanted to get his vicarious car jollies through me, I'd be glad to go along with the gag—I was sorry now I'd scared him away from the Mercedes lot, but I'd try to make it up to him. I prepared to get rabidly excited about Beamers. Maybe I'd even insist on driving a Jaguar. If there was a Rolls in Monterey County, I might take it for a spin.

But I did have one needle to deliver. "Esperanza told me you're such a reverse snob, you won't even get an answering machine."

"Rebecca, read my lips. I am from the Southland, where we worship the automobile. We're talking religion here."

"Praise Henry Ford and pass the cellular phone."

"But Esperanza's damn right about those dumb machines. A stupid toy for stupid people who keep hoping someone will have something interesting to say to them sometime."

"That's certainly what I hope when I play my messages. You sound like someone from another century."

"Only in certain areas. I'll tell you something—as soon as I can afford a nice car, I *am* getting a phone for it." He gave me his million-dollar smile. "It's the L.A. way."

He led me over to a metallic-finish convertible, some-where between bronze and silver, very discreet, very profes-sional.

"This one might do," I said.

Julio was walking around it, admiring from all angles. He patted it. "Gorgeous little 325I, aren't you, baby?" His tone had turned to baby talk. Sometimes I feel men and women will never begin to understand each other, and there's no point trying.

His hand still caressing the paint job, he looked back at me, reluctantly, I thought. "I really like these better than the 560 SLs, which would run you at least sixty-five. Little baby like this, you could probably get for thirty-five."

My knees turned to Jell-O. Humor him, I told myself. This whole adventure is for his amusement. It's nothing to do with you. "Let's look at it in red," I croaked.

"Are you getting a cold?" he said, but the late-arriving salesman, not nearly so Johnny-on-the-spot as Black Magic, had now caught up with us and sailed into his role: "Yes, ma'am, I've got one that's going to make you forget you ever heard the name Mercedes, Saab, Jaguar, anything else."

"Red?"

"Just like this one, only the color a fire engine gnashes its teeth and dreams about being."

The salesman was hardly taller than me, and wiry, dressed in an absurdly fashionable baggy suit, like something you'd wear to a South of Market night club but otherwise wouldn't be caught dead in. It was a shiny olive, with a small print in it. One lock of hair trailed down his silly-looking back, and his voice was shrill. It wouldn't have mattered if he'd looked like Jabba the Hut. Julio was hanging on every word, and the words had started to come with the speed of semiautomatic weapon fire. Me, I was more or less tuning out.

Idly I followed the two of them, mentally sketching a picture for a kid's book—a sleeping fire engine, closed eyes where its windshield should be, great gnashing teeth set into its hood. All the cars on the lot looked pretty much alike to me. That is, they did until I spotted one that looked different. Very different. Somebody's trade-in probably.

It looked entirely out of place on that lot, exuding as it did a quiet dignity yet earthy charm. It was a car that looked like it could go anywhere, indeed practically seemed to be in motion already, though it was just sitting there lording it over the Beamers. If you scratched the paint, it wouldn't be a major tragedy, it would just give it more character, as if it needed any. This was a car with the character of a stagecoach or a hansom cab, maybe even the Orient Express. *And* it was a convertible every bit as snappy as those little 325s.

I stopped dead.

"Rebecca? What is it?"

"I didn't know they came in white."

"White? Why not white? We've got every color you can name and then some. *Sure* they come in white," said the salesman.

I walked, as if in a trance, toward the car I knew I had to have.

"Rebecca!" shouted Julio. "That's a Jeep!"

He was so enraged, I would have feared for his sanity if he hadn't explained about the car sect he belonged to.

"That," I said, "is a chariot." And he saw that I was a lost cause.

Due to one thing and another regarding the surprise of love at first sight and my lack of cash on hand for such an eventuality, I couldn't actually drive the Jeep out of the place that day. But I drove it around for about half an hour before I could bear to say good-bye, and by the end of the test-drive, Julio had come around. He sat beside me singing the theme from "Rawhide" and cracking an imaginary whip at nonexistent dogies, which may have been meant to annoy me, but ended up getting both of us caught up in the pioneer spirit of the thing. The salesman sulked in the backseat.

Back in Julio's car, I was so exhilarated, I threw my arms around him and ended up in a serious lip-lock.

"See you tonight?" he said.

"Yes." No question. Absolutely.

I picked up my rented car at the aquarium, stopping first at the American Tin Cannery. There was a lingerie outlet there. After a small but satisfactory shopping spree, I headed for Carmel.

Katy's maid was a loose end I needed to tie up. She met me at the door of her little house with a face swollen from crying and an air that was frankly eager. Her belongings were strewn everywhere as she attempted to pack, extremely inefficiently it looked like, distracted by grief. She seemed glad to see someone, anyone.

I explained my errand and was told I must not call her "Yolie," that only Katy had done that, that it reminded her too much of the woman who had been her employer for fifteen years. Her name was Yolanda Estevez, she said, all very formally, but even in her sadness, I could see why Ricky had called her a "great old gal."

She was pushing sixty, probably, and she carried a lot of weight, but she wasn't fat; she was motherly. A serene, gracious kind of mother who'd probably raised seven or eight kids of her own before taking on one nearly her own age. That she had taken care of Katy in ways an adult didn't usually need was obvious from her conversation. I can't say I was surprised. Anyone who drank as much as Katy apparently needed a mother.

She wore a simple blouse and skirt that went well with a simple hairdo—her hair was almost shoulder-length, naturally curly and becoming. Occasionally she touched the front of her skirt, as if wiping her hands on an apron, but she wore no apron today. It was obviously the habit of a lifetime, and it brought to mind the aromas of baking bread and bubbling sauces.

The little house Ricky had remodeled had been fixed up with pillows and plants—modest things—but it was a comfortable place to be, or would have been if not for the disarray. Clearly Yolanda had the knack of making you feel comfortable and cared for.

Distractedly she continued packing as we talked, but her heart wasn't in it. She made practically no progress, and I could see she was doing it only because it kept at least a part of her mind off Katy.

"I feel like I had my arm chopped off," she said. "I been with Katy so long, I don't know what to do without her."

"It must be awful for you."

"They say she was beaten. They say someone beat her before they strangled her. They beat my poor, delicate, beautiful Katy."

"Ohhhh." Involuntarily I let the noise out. I had put the horrible image of Katy's pathetic, beaten body out of my mind. Yolanda's words brought it back.

"What is it, baby?"

"I saw her. Ricky found her body and he called me before the police."

Yolanda stopped her aimless packing and sat down. "You poor child."

"I know this is hard for you."

"For so many years I love her like a daughter. I do everything for her—I cook, I wake her up and get her to bed when she fall asleep somewhere else, I remember her appointments, I get her ready to go." Her arm made a wide sweep. "Everything."

"You two must have been very close."

She nodded, blinking tears.

"Do you think you're up to answering a few questions?"

"Chure."

"Do you know the Sheffield Pearl?"

"Chure."

"Ricky says you were here the night she showed it to him—do you remember that?"

"She give it to him, I think."

"Did you see her give it to him?"

She shook her head. "No, but she give it away twice before. To two other men. She asked me later if she give it to Ricky. She forget sometime." She frowned and tapped her forehead.

"You were here Friday?"

"Tha's when all that happen. She get a phone call from somebody asking about the pearl."

"She did? Did you answer the phone?"

"No, but Katy tell me about it. First, she send me to see if the pearl was missing. I go look and say it is. Then she get off the phone and she say, 'Yolie, the pearl couldn't have been stolen, could it?' I say, no, I bet you give it to Ricky. She say, 'I *knew* it couldn't have been,' and snaps her fingers like she remember she did give it to Ricky."

"Did she say who the caller was?"

"No. I don' think it was Ricky, though. If she give him the pearl, he wouldn't tell her it was stolen, would he?"

"Is that what the caller said?"

"Tha's what I think he said."

"He? Was it a man?"

"Lemme see." She closed her eyes and thought for a few minutes. "I don't know. Katy didn't say, one way or the other."

"I wonder. Did you know Sadie Swedlow? Could it have been her?"

At the mention of her name, Yolanda teared up again. "Oh, Sadie! Sadie die, too, the minute I leave town. They both die."

It was no good reminding her that she'd been out of town every weekend of her life and they hadn't died then. I asked again, "Could she have been the caller?"

Yolanda shrugged, her large shoulders heaving, the gesture meant to work off some of her hurt as much as anything else, I thought. "I guess so," she said.

"What time did the call come in?"

"Late afternoon. Four, five, six. I don' know. Seven, maybe. Night looks like afternoon this time of year."

"But you must know. You left Friday night. Was it just before you left or earlier?"

"I lef' Saturday morning. The las' time I saw Katy was Saturday morning." Her voice was so thick with held-back tears I didn't have the heart to go on.

The fog came in as I drove back to Monterey, lowering the temperature, dampening the air. I usually enjoy fog, find it exhilarating rather than ominous. But I got an eerie feeling on that drive, as if things had suddenly slipped very much out of kilter. I found myself driving erratically.

My heart was beating fast and, despite the cold, I was sweating; my mind kept slipping in and out of gear. The car, not surprisingly, nearly slipped off the road. I skidded and braked and finally brought it back under control, but in a much-sobered condition—either the brakes were going or I really shouldn't be driving right now. I slowed down as much as I dared and, rolling into the Pelican Inn at almost a crawl, couldn't be sure whether the brakes or I was the problem. Probably I was. I was shaking.

I peeled off my clothes and stood in the shower for twenty minutes or more, rivulets running off my hair and into my face, trying to figure out what was wrong with me, why I had so much invested, why I should care so much, and whether I was simply being silly.

In the end, I called Julio and said I was very sorry, I couldn't make it, I had an emergency. I called a cab—I didn't trust myself in the damn rented car again—and pulled on jeans and a red turtleneck while I waited for it.

CHAPTER 17

Libby answered the door, but she was so engrossed in some TV show, she barely gave me a cursory hug. Familiarity, I surmised, was breeding the usual thing.

From upstairs, Marty hollered, "Rebecca? Come up a minute."

She was getting ready to go out.

"Date night again?" It's possible there was the slightest irritated edge to my voice. Marty as sweetheart of the rodeo was getting to me.

"Committee meeting," she said, seeming not to notice. I sat on her bed as she tried on a belt, discarded it, tried on another. Perhaps she had a date after the committee meeting. Or maybe Jim Lambert was on the committee, whatever it was. I didn't care; in fact, I had a feeling the less I knew about her personal life, the better.

"Is Keil baby-sitting?"

"No, he's over at a friend's. I'm taking Libby to her dad's before I go." She turned away from the mirror and stared at me. "Listen, I'm running late and I have to stop by the aquarium on the way. You couldn't run her over there, could you?"

"Sorry. I came in a taxi."

"Oh. Just to visit?"

"No. I need to know something. I just talked to Katy Montebello's maid. She said you called Katy on Friday. In fact, she told me a very interesting story about your call."

Once again she abandoned the endless fascination of her own reflection to look me full in the face. "What are you talking about? I don't even know Katy Montebello."

I said sweetly. "Give me a break, please. We talked about her."

She resumed her mascara application. "I know we talked about her, Rebecca. But I didn't say she was my bosom buddy. I didn't call her Friday and I've never called her."

"Are you familiar with the Sheffield Pearl?"

"Sure. Everyone around here knows about it. About every six months the local paper does a write-up on Katy, or she puts the pearl on exhibit at some benefit, and that gets written up. Nobody doesn't know about it—why?"

"How about Sadie? She was new in town—would she know about it?"

"I don't know. Maybe not. How do I look?"

"Fine." Ordinary. As usual. "Marty, on Friday night— the night Sadie died—you went out and came back after your date with Jim, right?"

"Right. I had to meet you." She started to rummage through her closet and now pulled out a white blazer, which she shrugged into. "This?"

"It washes you out. You're a summer, I think. How about something pastel?" I heard myself nattering on, realizing exactly how silly I sounded, and wished I had more fashion advice I could use to avoid getting on with it.

"Oh." She rummaged again. "Maybe I can have it dyed."

"Marty, as you were leaving, did you see Julio leaving, too?"

"Julio?" She held up a light blue jacket. "How about this?"

"It's fine. Did you see Julio?"

"I don't think so. I can't remember."

If he had left when Marty did, when he said he did, then that argued that he hadn't been the one who had taken her letter opener and windbreaker. It didn't prove anything, but it seemed to make sense that the murderer wouldn't have drowned Sadie, then left the building for some reason, then come back to set up the frame. And as long as Marty had been there, so, probably, had her jacket and letter opener.

Oh, damn! It suddenly hit me that they could have been taken in advance, for a premeditated murder. I'd been imagining one of passion.

Try as I might, I couldn't get Julio off the hook in my own mind. Here was the scenario that played on my mental movie screen on the foggy drive back to Monterey:

Sometime Friday, probably before six o'clock, Sadie talked to Julio about Esperanza, but contrary to his story, she did show him the pearl. He thought he recognized it and understood its worth. He stole it, either calling Katy first to verify its authenticity or calling her later to see if she'd pay a reward for its return. However, Sadie, having told no one else about the pearl, accused him of stealing it and he killed her. But Marty saw him leaving the roof, and Warren saw him in the parking lot. To cover himself, he invented the story he'd told me.

The call to Katy had me going—because Julio's story certainly rang true in one respect. Everyone I'd talked to—except Marty—had loved Sadie. Sadie was universally thought to be a wonderful person and clearly adored by children. So she would have kept Esperanza's secret. She would have told no one about the pearl—probably not even Julio, but he was the one person she might have told, in an effort to get Esperanza out of trouble.

There in the safety of Marty's utterly uninspired bedroom, it sounded far-fetched. I thought maybe I'd worked myself into a lather about Julio's guilt because I was really just nervous about going out with him. But what was I, a teenager?

Certainly not, I told myself. I was an adult woman, temporarily too smitten to remember she shouldn't date a murder suspect. It had taken a strange twist of the paranoia mechanism to avert a near-error. Good judgment had been restored. Fine.

"Time to go," said Marty. "I don't have time to drop you at your hotel, but I could take you to the aquarium. You're near there, aren't you? You could walk or get a taxi, I guess."

"Thanks."

I thought I would walk. It was a nice night and I'd stop for a bite along the way. I didn't dare drive the rented car again. I might go to a movie if I happened to stroll past a theater. I needed to be out, so that if Julio called I wouldn't know about it. My talk with Marty hadn't cleared up anything.

I would have gone right away, but Libby wanted to look at the fish while her mom did her errand, and she wanted me for company. Frankly, I was delighted to be wanted.

"See you in a minute," said Marty. "I've got to get something out of my office."

There was apparently a party that night, and we'd arrived with the caterers. They were busily making a Mexican village out of the first floor of the aquarium, setting up cardboard arches, bringing in cacti, hauling around cases of Corona and Dos Equis. I wondered if mariachis were booked, and if so, how the fish would like the music. Probably they wouldn't be fazed. Mine had to put up with my piano playing.

Innocent Libby, of course, had never seen the kelp tank as I'd seen it last. I wasn't even sure she knew that was where her mom and I found Sadie. So I didn't want to let on I thought it would be hard to look at it again, hard not to think of the shark caught in Sadie's panty hose, the yellow beaks darting ruthlessly toward their prey. But the flashbacks lasted only a moment. The swaying kelp, the insouciant fish swimming so confidently, the gorgeous invertebrates—the starfish, the anemones—worked their usual magic almost immediately. As always, I was mesmerized.

"Rebecca, look!" Libby was pointing to a sandy area where nothing had been planted.

I stared, having no idea what I was looking for. There were a million things worth looking at in that tank. What had caught her ten-year-old fancy?

"Look at what?"

"Look over there—way in the back of that little sandy patch."

Did I see a sand dollar, almost buried? There sure wasn't anything else, not even a lazy rockfish swimming through.

"I'm looking, I'm looking."

"Don't you see anything?"

"What am I looking for?"

"The pearl! There it is!"

It was one of those things—whether the eye or the brain plays the trick, I'm not sure, but once I saw the pearl, I couldn't see how I could have failed to see it before. It looked so natural, so much at home, as if it had rolled out of a cache of pirates' treasure and settled there in the sand a century ago. I had taken it for a rock.

Now I saw that it looked a lot like a brain, and at the same time undeniably like a pearl the size of a Ping-Pong ball. I was reminded of Poe's purloined letter—unless you knew exactly where to look and what you were looking for, you'd never see it lying right there in plain sight.

No one would have hidden it there except someone who could easily retrieve it later—someone who was a good diver and had access to the kelp tank. My stomach fluttered.

"What are we going to do, Rebecca? We can't tell my mom. She'll know Esperanza stole it."

"I know. We won't tell her. But it's okay to tell the police now. They already know about it."

She raised her head, searching my face with panicked eyes.

"It's okay," I said. "Esperanza's not going to get in trouble."

"She's not?"

"She didn't tell you about it?"

She shook her head. "She's sleeping over tomorrow. We were going to talk then."

"I'll let her tell the details."

Her face lit up with an idea. "You mean Julio knows about it now?"

I nodded.

"And he's not mad at her?"

"Well, not real mad, anyhow."

"He could get it out of there. Why don't we just tell Julio?"

Her innocence was heart-wrenching. "Sweetheart, it'll be all right. Believe me. But we really do have to call the police."

Her face clouded and pinched up, as she tried to hold back tears of worry for her friend. I felt tears spring to my own eyes—there was something so moving about watching such a small organism trying to muddle its way through life. It was hard enough when you had a couple of degrees and a driver's license.

"I'll go right now, honey. You stay here and wait for your mom."

I was about to head toward the phone at the reception desk—the same one Marty had used Friday night—when I heard Marty somewhere up above.

"Warren Nowell, I've got a few things to say to you!"

She was descending the stairs from the second floor, face contorted. Warren, the object of her anger, was walking toward Libby and me, having apparently just come from the restaurant or the bookstore.

Marty was waving her desk calendar and another slip of paper at him—the note about her date, I was sure.

"What was this doing in your desk?"

"Oh, hi, Marty," said Warren, as if nothing were wrong. He was adapting beautifully to his new role as a leader of men and women. Beside his sangfroid, Marty's anger looked childish. "Hi, Rebecca. Libby." He ruffled Libby's hair.

Marty had reached the rest of us by now. "What did you mean going through my desk?"

"I took some things out for safekeeping. I knew you'd be gone a few days. I was trying to help, that's all."

She looked at her watch. "You weren't, damn you. God, I'm late, thanks to you—I had to search your desk as well as mine—and I still have to drop Libby off. . . ."

Time, time, time. It seemed all she ever thought about. I loved the way she'd simply dropped the idea that she'd "had to" search his desk, as if such trespasses were an everyday occurrence.

"Let me," said Warren. "Is she going to Don's? I'll be happy to drop her. Can I drop you, too, Rebecca?"

Marty said. "I'll almost forgive you if you'll do that."

He smiled. "Glad to. That is, if nobody minds waiting a minute. I've got to get something from my office."

Right. He probably wanted to lock his desk.

Marty was all smiles, too. Why not? She'd won. She had her things back. "By the way," she said, "how did your meeting go?"

"You knew about it, did you?"

"Of course, Warren. I knew I might have to search your desk. I picked a time when you'd be busy."

And she would have sashayed off in semi-triumph if

Libby hadn't wailed, "Mo-o-m! My backpack's in the car."

All three of them scattered, leaving me with the fish and the caterers.

CHAPTER 18

If I called the police now, they might make me wait for them. But if I called from the Pelican Inn, they'd come to me there. The pearl could wait another ten minutes.

Libby came back first, looking slightly forlorn.

Warren arrived a few minutes later, now with his briefcase. "Everybody ready? Let's go."

As we drove up to the motel, he glanced at his watch. "I'd better call Mary Ellen—the meeting took longer than I thought. Could I use your phone, Rebecca?"

The two of us got out and Libby stayed. Warren said, "Why don't you come in? I might be a few minutes."

Oh, great. Just what Libby and I needed—an impromptu party with a self-important, just-promoted hunk of passivity suddenly converted to Type A. He was probably going to make business calls with an audience.

He brought his briefcase in, no doubt containing a sheaf of messages he simply had to return before he could even take Libby home.

Libby said, "Can I go to the bathroom?" and headed toward it.

Warren picked up the phone before I could even see if my message light was flashing, but he didn't dial, just checked it out; for what, I didn't know.

He started to rummage in his briefcase. Oh, well, this was

obviously going to take forever. I picked up a T-shirt and started to fold it.

"Turn around slowly," said Warren. His voice sounded higher now, slightly excited, I thought, stretched to cover something unusual.

He was pointing a spear gun at me.

"This is what I went back for," he said.

The toilet flushed.

He held out one hand. "Walk toward me."

Feeling like a sleepwalker, I did. When I was close enough, he grabbed my arm, roughly, and held me in front of him, the spear gun close to my rib cage. Libby came out of the bathroom.

"It's all right," I said, hating myself for lying so egregiously.

Her eyes were blue Frisbees. "What's happening?"

"Rebecca is going to tie you up," said Warren.

"No!" Libby and I spoke together.

"Yes," said Warren, his mouth turning up at the corners. He was smiling. "Sit on the bed, Libby."

Silently she obeyed. He pulled me closer, then heaved me onto the bed and grabbed Libby's arm, squeezing.

"Ouch!"

"Don't touch her!"

"Rebecca." He spoke with the air of a doctor addressing a mental patient. "Don't be stupid. You do what I say or I'll hurt her."

I didn't move; couldn't. Could this be happening?

"You saw Katy, didn't you?"

Was he confessing to killing her? I couldn't ask him in front of Libby.

Yes, I'd seen Katy; and if Warren had killed her, that wasn't all he'd done to her. I said, "What do you want me to tie her with?"

Libby gasped, betrayed.

"The curtain ties," he said. "First close the curtains very tight. And that's how you're going to tie this young lady. Very tight. You're going to pull the ties until the circulation stops at her wrists."

Libby turned terrified, unbelieving eyes on me. I couldn't bear to look at her. I got up to get the ties. When I came back, Warren let go of Libby's arm and moved a few feet away, the spear gun aimed at Libby's heart.

"Rebecca, look at me."

Glad to. So long as I didn't have to look at the ten-year-old who was shaking now, trembling like Esperanza freshly fished from the bay, falling apart before my seemingly heartless eyes. Looking at him as ordered, I put an arm around Libby, pulled her close to me. Instinctively she molded her body to mine like a toddler does, suddenly regressed to a small being used to using adult bodies for comfort. Holding her like that, feeling her panic, understanding that I was her only hope, I felt waves of nausea starting. I wanted to throw my body on top of hers in case the world exploded.

I put my hand to my mouth. "I'm going to throw up."

"Do it then."

I stared to heave, to go into the bathroom, but Warren said, "Here."

I leaned toward the floor, heaving. Nothing came up, just waves and waves of painful heaves. Noisy ones. Libby must have thought I was dying. Finally the nausea stopped. But Warren kept going in and out of focus.

"You do exactly as I say, or I swear I will fire a spear into the left side of her skinny chest."

Libby's hand covered her heart. I said, "I believe you. I know what you're capable of."

He backhanded me, so hard my teeth clicked together. I hit Libby's head with mine and heard her sharp intake of breath. We toppled together into a quivering pile.

Warren said, "You don't know shit."

When he had come close, I'd smelled something ugly. He was perspiring heavily, but this wasn't a perspiration odor. Perhaps it was fear, the famous fear that animals are supposed to be able to smell, but I didn't think so. I thought it was something that came out of Warren's pores when he was excited, not a sexual odor, but something musky, and it dawned on me that he was enjoying himself.

From my toes to my scalp, fury rose, a palpable current, and I felt my focus come back, white-hot, single-minded. All right. It was up to me to get Libby out of this. I would.

"Tie her wrists behind her back."

I didn't have the heart to cut off her circulation. Even so, I tied the cord so tight I had to bite my lip to keep from crying out when I pulled it.

"Let me see," said Warren.

"Get up, sweetheart, and turn around."

She stood, turned, and quickly sat down again.

Warren moved forward very slowly. He whapped not me but Libby this time, very deliberately and not very hard, just a little slap that made a nasty pop. The nausea started, but this time I swallowed it. I couldn't afford to lose control again.

"Tighter."

I tied her wrists tighter, now biting the insides of my cheeks to keep from screaming and flying at him. She was whimpering steadily.

"Tie her feet with the other one."

I couldn't bear to lay her down like a roped calf. I let her sit, and sat on the floor to tie her ankles.

"My dad's expecting me," she said. "I have to call my dad."

Damn! If she was missed, we might have a chance.

But Warren only smiled. He'd already thought it out. "No,

you don't. Rebecca will do that. You know Don, don't you, Rebecca?''

I nodded, not sure where this was leading.

As if the mention of it had brought it to life, the phone rang, making me jump.

"Nervous, Rebecca?"

"A little."

"Answer it and act normal. Find out who it is and say you'll call right back. Then hang up and report to me. Got it?''

I nodded.

"You better do this right." He moved to the bed and trained the spear gun on Libby.

I lifted the phone. "Rebecca, are you all right?" It was Julio.

"Fine, Julio." My voice was as bright and cheery as if I were at a party. Damn the acting lessons! "Listen, I just stepped out of the shower. Can I call you right back?"

"Sure."

I hung up.

Warren said, "Julio," a fresh smile playing at the corners of his mouth. "You're fucking him, aren't you?"

"Of course not. We're just friends." I glanced at Libby. It was crazy, but I was upset that he'd used the F-word in her hearing.

"Friends." He leered.

"Warren, I have to tell you I'm really offended by your language."

He put the spear gun in his lap and roared. Maybe I could get it. . . .

But I couldn't—he kept a tight grip even as he laughed his nerdy head off. "Offended by my language!"

When the joke wore thin, he turned serious, nasty. "Call him back, Rebecca. Make a date with him. For now."

"Julio?"

"Julio?" He mimicked me. "Of course Julio. And quit playing dumb."

I reached for the phone book, but Libby reeled off the number. As I dialed, Warren said, "One more thing: Tell him to order a pizza, but leave it there. If he wants you to meet him anywhere, say your car's broken. He's got to come here. Got that?"

I nodded.

"Oh, yeah, and one other thing. Call Don first."

"Shall I say she'll be a little late?"

"Say you and Julio are taking his kid on an overnight camping trip. And Libby wants to go."

Don answered on the first ring, even his "hello" sounding nervous. She was late. He was waiting by the phone. He wanted her home, argued with me. I finally had to tell him we'd already gone, I was calling from Big Sur. Hearing me, Libby started to cry.

Seeing her convulsed, sobbing her heart out, I made on-the-spot plans to kill Warren, and I believe I could have done it, but he grabbed my free hand and twisted it behind me as soon as I'd set the receiver down.

He tossed me aside, into a chair. For a moment he seemed at a loss. He surveyed the room while I breathed heavily. Libby continued to sob.

"Find a sock," he said. "And gag her."

I found the sock and sat on the edge of the bed, but I could go no further. "I can't do it."

He touched the spear to Libby's eye. "You'd rather she go blind?"

God, it was horrible. When I was a kid, I held my dog while the vet put him to sleep, and it wasn't as bad as stuffing the sock. Not by a long shot.

"Okay. Call Julio now."

I was shaking, didn't think I could do it. But I did, palms sweaty, voice steady—a regular Sarah Bernhardt.

"Pizza?" he said when I got to that part. As I hung up, I heard him say again, "Pizza?"

Maybe the pizza would make him suspicious. More likely he'd just think I'd forgotten we didn't eat pizza together.

CHAPTER 19

With the cord from a lamp, Warren tied my ankles together, cutting off the circulation. I had no idea why he didn't tie my hands. He experimented until he had the tableau he wanted for Julio. Me sitting on the bed in view of the door; he and Libby in chairs just out of sight, the chairs touching, the spear gun at Libby's heart. When twenty minutes had passed, he unlocked the door.

I tried to think.

Warren sweated and delivered a monologue about how hungry he was. He rifled my luggage and purse for food, finally coming up with menthol-eucalyptus cough drops, not a wimpy snack. He chewed loudly. I thought I saw him pocket something from my makeup kit, but I couldn't see what.

It was another twenty minutes before Julio arrived.

"Come in," I called, following orders. I had my legs curled behind me, hiding my bound ankles. I stretched out an inviting arm, once again as ordered.

Maybe I'm beautiful when I'm terrified. Or maybe the pose really was as sexy as Warren apparently thought it was. Without a word, Julio strode over, gathered me up, and began kissing me as if there were no tomorrow. Which I was beginning to think there might not be.

I didn't respond, which should have been some sort of clue, but the scene on the beach must have left him frustrated. He didn't stop until Warren said, "Hello, Julio."

He dropped me, spinning toward the voice.

Warren was not only smiling, but looking like a man who's just finished dinner at someplace like Stars or Oliveto and can still taste chocolate and cognac. "Sit down or I'll kill her." He nodded at Libby.

He turned back to me. I had to look at the second face that day that said I'd betrayed it. I uncurled my legs to show my feet, now swollen from their bonds.

"What the hell is going on?"

Warren tossed me another lamp cord. "Rebecca, tie his hands." And then I knew why he hadn't tied my wrists.

When I was done, Warren asked me to come to him. I had to drop off the bed and slither like a snake. When I arrived, he made me turn around, facing Julio. He wrapped his legs around my body, holding me down, digging his heels into my abdomen, and holding me by the hair. This time, for Julio's benefit, he brought out a new weapon—my nail scissors, taken from my makeup bag.

"Later tonight I'm going to be asking you to do something for me," he said. "And while you're doing it, I'm going to keep Rebecca and Libby with me. I'm showing you these so that you'll understand what we'll be doing while you're busy." He took the scissors and started to jab them into my eye. Julio lunged. "Don't do that." Warren raked my face. I felt the sting and the wet of the scratch. Involuntarily I made a little sound. "Ohh. Just like Libby. I guess we'll have to stuff you, too. Bring me a sock."

I slithered till I found one, brought it back, and let him stuff my mouth. Julio's rage filled the room, thick as motor oil. I could feel it, erratic and dangerous, building steam.

"Now back to business, Rebecca, dear. Close your eyes."

Julio tensed. It was as if someone had played a high-frequency note that wouldn't stop.

"I'm going to give you an eyelash trim."

From my end, it wasn't so bad. Not being able to see the

scissors, I hadn't a sense of sharp-pointed things close to my face. In fact, it was kind of a relief to be able to tune Warren out for a few minutes. But from Libby's whimpering and Julio's heavy breathing, I guess watching was a little nervous-making.

"Open your eyes now." I obeyed. "You're ugly, Rebecca. That really made you ugly."

I nodded in a way that I hoped he'd find properly submissive. Who cared if I was ugly?

To Julio he said, "You know, I really enjoyed that."

"You're sick."

"Yes. Before we leave here, I want to make sure you know who you're dealing with. I have killed two people and I enjoyed it. I will kill more if I need to. I just want you to know that. We're leaving now. Rebecca will drive. You will ride in the front seat with her. I will ride in the back with Libby. It would give me the greatest pleasure to shoot this child through the heart and watch her die."

My ears rang. Dear God, he couldn't be saying that.

"If I see that you have jeopardized my chances, I have nothing to lose by killing her—and I will have the pleasure of claiming a third victim. Is that clear?"

Julio said, "Warren, you don't sound like yourself."

I didn't know him well, but that was my impression, too. He sounded pompous and professorial. I didn't realize he had such presence, could be so sure of himself.

Warren said, "I'm not myself, Julio. I have come into my own."

"Where are we going?"

"Your house, of course. But one question. Where is Esperanza?"

"At Amber's. Sleeping over."

She was safe. It was something to hang on to.

Warren ungagged me, untied my ankles, and let me rub

them awhile before attempting to drive. They hurt a lot. While I recovered, he ripped out the phone.

"Rebecca, pick Libby up. We're going in your car."

"I need my keys."

He searched my purse, tossed it over.

He made Julio walk ahead and get in the shotgun seat. Then he got in the back with Libby, holding the spear gun on her, as I walked around to my side, and started the car.

When we arrived, he made me tie Julio's ankles, and then he tied me, wrists and ankles. He sat us on Julio's pathetic couch, and then, taking Libby and the spear gun for insurance, went on a tour of the house. He came back pointing a revolver.

"Shit!" said Julio. "My mama told me not to buy that thing."

"Cut the conversation. Where's the pizza?"

"Pizza?" said Julio. "I thought that was a joke. Rebecca and I—"

"You didn't get the pizza?"

"No."

"You idiot!" He slapped Julio's face with the pistol. Libby made an animal sound. "I was going to ungag her," he said. "But you can forget that now."

Warren went into the kitchen.

"Warren! I could make you something."

He came back with chips and salsa, stuffing them into his mouth mechanically. "You can cook, Rebecca?"

"Some things." The salsa gave me an idea. "How about *huevos rancheros*?"

"So you can cook, can you? Very interesting."

"Shall I make you something fabulous?"

He looked at his watch. "Oh, by all means. But not yet. We have to go out again—as soon as the party's over."

That had a nasty sound to it. "What party?" I asked.

"The one at the aquarium. What do you think this charade's about?"

For a long time he didn't say another word—just stared into space. That was okay. He wasn't torturing Libby.

But after a while, she began making urgent noises in her throat.

"What does she want?"

"Why don't you ask her?"

He pulled the gag out. For a moment Libby didn't speak, seemed to be adjusting to the feeling of having her mouth to herself. Warren said, "What is it, kid?"

"I have to go to the bathroom."

"Wee-wee in your pants."

I had a weird sense of déjà vu. There was something familiar, but I couldn't think what.

I said, "I have to go, too. Shall I wee-wee in *my* pants?" I was being deliberately crude, hoping to gross him out.

He grimaced. "All right, all right, you can both go. You, too, Julio?"

Julio shook his head.

He left Julio where he was, untied my feet and Libby's. At the bathroom door, he untied Libby's hands and told her to go while we watched, the gun trained on my ear.

Cheeks flaming, she turned slightly away so at least he couldn't see her face. When it was my turn, I took a different approach. I stared at him as I unzipped, not sexual, just boldly immodest. Then I dropped my drawers and pretended to examine them.

I cried out in high alarm, "Oh, yuck, I've got my period! Jesus, what a mess."

The man who could stick a letter opener in another person's eye and apparently not bat his own practically turned pea-green before my eyes.

"I've got to get a Tampax."

"Shut up and pee."

"Warren. I'm not kidding. I've really got to. It's going to be all over my jeans, on Julio's couch. . . ." I held up a piece of toilet paper, thinking chances were good he'd never find out there was nothing more revolting on it than a saccharine flower design. "Look at that."

I was right. He averted his eyes. "Okay, okay."

"I've got spares in my purse."

"Go get them."

I got up and started to waddle, jeans around my ankles. "Pull up your pants, goddammit!"

I complied, virtually hearing the creak of wheels as he tried to figure a way to avoid witnessing unimaginable grossness, yet keep me in sight. I made a big show of tearing off a wad of toilet paper and stuffing it in my panties to catch the overflow.

Warren brought Libby with us to find my purse, keeping her covered while I rummaged for the Tampax. While my hands were out of sight in the purse, I took three of Mickey's Seconal capsules—all I had left—out of my plastic pill container and stuck them under the sleeve of my turtleneck.

Triumphantly I extracted a tampon, waving it in his face. He looked as if he were witnessing ritual butchery.

Good.

When he'd destroyed the last of the chips and salsa, he glanced again at his watch. "Time to go. The travel arrangements will be the same. Only this time I will be threatening Little Miss Muffet with this example of modern weaponry." He waved the gun. "She'll go first; then Rebecca; then Julio. All three of you will be dead in about five seconds if anything untoward happens."

He sure was talking peculiarly—like a schoolteacher. His mother had been one; maybe he'd picked up the habit from her.

Suddenly I remembered the story Ricky had told me and

realized what the déjà vu was about. Like mother like son, I guessed. She sounded bonkers, and Warren certainly was.

Before we left, he filled up the bathtub. And then he hunted up a plastic trash bag to bring along.

Mercifully, he untied Libby's feet before we left, and slung one of Esperanza's jackets around her shoulders, hiding her tied hands. Julio, too, was given a shoulder-draped jacket. I was untied for driving.

The aquarium seemed nearly deserted, though it's never completely so, I'd learned the other night. There are always security guards at the very least, and lots of people work late. This part of the operation would depend partly on luck— whether ours or Warren's remained to be seen.

We slipped in the back door and behind the scenes to aquarist territory. "To the dive lockers," said Warren.

He opened Julio's locker, tossed his equipment on the floor, and had me pick it up. Then we all took the elevator to the roof. The lights weren't on.

"Could I ask what this is all about?" asked Julio. "Because I've got the feeling you're going to send me down there, and I can't go in the dark."

"Yeah, you can ask. Suit up while I tell you. Rebecca, untie him."

Warren kept the gun trained on him, not letting his eyes stray for a millisecond, as Julio undressed and put on the wet suit. The irony of the situation wasn't lost on me—this was my first look at a very fine body I wanted to live to see naked again.

"You know what the Sheffield Pearl is?"

"Yes." Julio stiffened.

"Ever seen it?"

"I can't remember; I've seen so many pictures of it. . . ."

"Good enough. It's down there. And you're going to get it."

"That's what all the killing is about? That's what you're threatening us for right now? That ugly thing?"

"No," said Warren. "That isn't what it's about at all. It's just a loose end I have to tie up. We don't want any loose ends, do we?"

Julio sighed. "Could we have some light, please?"

"I'm afraid not. That wouldn't be keeping a very low profile. But Libby and Rebecca have seen it. They'll tell you where it is."

Libby said, "Near the round window. You know that little sandy place? Near the back."

"Can you manage okay?" I said.

"That area's small. I can just rake it with my hands till I find it." He spoke to Warren. "But it's a long way down. You'll have to give me plenty of time."

"Just remember one thing. I'm up here with Rebecca, Libby, and a gun. And these." He displayed the nail scissors.

With a soft splash, Julio went over the side. Warren took us into the rooftop lab to wait. I knew he'd taken us inside because he didn't want to encounter a guard. He could explain our presence with no trouble—after all, he was acting head of the institution. But I knew he didn't want to be the last person seen with us.

He drummed his fingers. "Rebecca, you got any more cough drops?"

I shook my head.

"I'm starving." He started to range about the lab, opening cabinets. I feared for the baby invertebrates—he might decide to eat them raw. But he didn't lapse into such lack of professionalism, though he seemed to have dropped his pedantic speech mode.

I was glad he'd found something to occupy his mind. With the sadistic streak he had, I was afraid he'd decide to pull Julio up too fast just to watch him get the bends. In fact, I was very much afraid of that.

I sat down and took Libby in my lap, an action Warren allowed, I surmised, because it occupied both of us and guaranteed neither would make sudden moves.

"Did you kill Sadie for the pearl?" I asked, more to keep him occupied than anything else.

"Of course not. Why would I care about the damned pearl?"

I could see it was going to be one of those conversations. Fortunately, Julio began to climb out of the tank, the creature from twenty thousand leagues, dark and alien in the moonlight.

Warren had me take the pearl and hand it over. He put Libby and me in front of him as Julio resumed his street clothes.

It had been a weird evening, but it got a lot weirder. Warren had Julio put water from the tank in the plastic bag we'd brought.

"Now," he said, "Let's get the puffers."

Julio stared.

"Don't just stand there, goddammit. Let's go get the puffers."

It still didn't seem to compute. "We're kidnapping the puffers?"

"Yeah. Maybe we'll hold them for ransom."

So we all trooped to the third floor while Julio got a net and transferred the fish to the bag. I could grasp the theory, sort of like the goldfish you buy in Baggies, but puffers were weird pets.

CHAPTER 20

When we'd put away the diving equipment, Warren retied Julio and forced him in the front seat again, but, wonder of wonders, he untied Libby. She was to have custody of the fish. Julio, who was supposed to be such a pal of marine animals, had been all for putting them in the trunk, but Warren was afraid they might get bruised. He was awfully particular about the damn puffers—and I had a bad feeling I knew what he wanted them for.

Warren said, "Rebecca, find a supermarket, will you? I could eat a Doberman." The guy was almost comical if you didn't know how dangerous he was.

All we could find was a 7-Eleven, but Warren went for it (after first making sure Julio already had the ingredients for *huevos rancheros*).

He took me with him, the gun out of sight in a coat pocket, digging into my hip. He'd issued one of his standard warnings. "Julio and Libby, leave the car or make a disturbance and your friend's a former lawyer. Got it?"

We got two six-packs of Pepsi, chips, bean dip, jalapeno-and-cheese dip, cookies, and salsa in a jar, Warren complaining like a kid that they didn't have the fresh kind.

As we paid, I looked out at the two in the car, hoping for signs of activity. Surely they could see what I could see: *This is it, guys. Probably our only chance. He's never going to*

*kill me in here. The worst he'll do is hold me hostage. Lean
on the horn, goddammit! Get us out of this!*

But you can't get good help anymore.

Libby waved. Just like Mom and Uncle Warren had popped
in for some TV snacks instead of our last meal on the planet.
Waved! I still can't get over it.

After we dumped the puffers in the bathtub, Warren said,
"Now. Food. Rebecca, get in that kitchen." He started mur-
dering chips and Pepsis the instant we were in there, but he
had great concentration. He could eat half a bag of chips
while tracking me like a man in love. The opportunity I
needed didn't materialize.

"I really can't tell you what a marvelous night it's been.
What a splendid four days, for that matter. Do you know you
three have really made my day?"

I said, "Why'd you kill Sadie, Warren? You said it had
nothing to do with the pearl—so what was it?"

He lifted a know-it-all finger. "Ah-ah, young lady, I said
no such thing. It had everything to do with the pearl. Just
not the usual thing."

"So are you going to tell us or not?" He was having such
a great time, I already knew the answer. Even if we didn't
want to know, we were going to.

But before he could get up a head of steam, I heard a funny
clicking sound—outside, I thought; running steps. Then the
familiar household sound of metal against metal—a key in
the door. It could be only one person.

"Run!" yelled Julio. "Esperanza, run for your life!"

Warren crossed the living room in three or four steps,
jerked the door open. Esperanza must have frozen. Warren
pulled her inside, fat fingers circling her upper arm, gun
pointed at her head. I could hear a car driving away.

Julio started to coo the usual dumb things: "It's all right,
baby. Everything's going to be—"

I could have cried.

"Shut up, Julio." Warren slapped Esperanza's face. "You've been a bad boy."

I flew out of the kitchen like a mother wolf, flung myself at Warren. Warren squeezed Esperanza's arm so tight, it turned red as I watched. He leveled the gun at the bridge of my nose. Esperanza screamed.

"Everybody cool out!"

He meant chill out; I prayed she wouldn't correct him.

She didn't. Everyone froze.

Finally I said, "Esperanza sometimes faints. Let her go, please."

He flung her into my arms. "What's happening?" she whispered.

I stroked her hair. How did you explain madness to a ten-year-old? "Why are you home?" I said.

"Amber got sick. We went to the emergency room and then Ricky dropped me off." She was still whispering.

Julio kept quiet, knowing, I suppose, that anything he said would be used against his daughter.

"Okay, okay, we're going to make a few changes. First, we tie up Esperanza." Warren tied her to a chair with some clothesline he must have found on his search. "And now, we hogtie Julio." He had me do it while he held the gun to Esperanza's temple. To make double sure, he didn't let me untie the wrists and ankles. I had to do the hog-tying above the other bonds, which had now turned Julio's skin an ugly purple.

Pretty soon it became clear why he was doing it—he was going to amuse himself with the rest of us, and he was afraid of Julio, even tied up.

That meant he wasn't all that much afraid of me, which might be good. I had a secret weapon now. When Julio yelled and Warren left me alone, I'd worked a Seconal into my palm, pulled the capsule apart, dumped the contents into the salsa for the *huevos*, and tucked the empty capsule halves back into my sleeve. With luck, the salsa would mask the taste.

My hands shook as I built the *huevos rancheros*. The eggs had finished poaching during the excitement, a good thing considering Warren's eagerness. It was all I could do to keep him at bay while I put together my version of the dish: the eggs served on a tortilla smeared with refried beans—in this case, bean dip—the whole thing topped with lots of salsa and tomatoes, then sour cream and cheese.

Warren retied me and ate standing at the counter.

"Excellent," he said. "You pass."

I nodded, humoring him.

"I think you're good enough to cook for the whole family. You hungry, Julio?"

Julio shook his head.

"I bet you kids are. And Rebecca's going to make you a lovely bouillabaisse, aren't you, Rebecca? Fugu bouillabaisse."

Fugu, of course, is another name for puffer.

"They say it makes great sashimi. If you eat only that, you're relatively safe. But you're going to eat everything—the liver, the skin, the intestines—all the yummy parts absolutely saturated in the world's deadliest nerve toxin."

The last of the *huevos* were disappearing. The man ate like most people breathe.

"We'll all watch our Rebecca fillet the fish, and then chop the onions and garlic—cooking for the people she loves, just a perfect little . . . What's the Yiddish word, Rebecca?"

"*Balabosta.*"

"And then we'll smell those delightful smells while it's cooking. Probably we won't smell them for long, though, because I bet you all four shit your pants thinking about what's in store. There are quite a few terrifying symptoms, but in the end, the toxin works by paralysis. You'll just freeze up, bit by bit, till you can't move. They say the victims retain acute mental consciousness till the last moment—no coma, no nothing.'' He yawned. ''Coffee time.''

I hoped that meant what I thought it did. He went into the kitchen, banged things around, and finally yelled, ''Esperanza, can you operate this goddamn coffee machine?''

He couldn't see us. I shook my head at her. ''No!'' she shouted.

''I can!'' I sang out sweetly. To the kids I whispered, ''Make noise in about ten minutes.''

He untied me and we went through the watching routine once more. I had to search for the coffee and then struggle to figure out the damned coffeemaker, but he barely noticed, he was so self-absorbed; back in lecture mode.

''The whole thing—the thing with Sadie—was a misunderstanding, you see. But a fortuitous error, it turned out. It changed everything.''

''Right. Now you're a homicidal maniac.'' I palmed another capsule.

''Homicidal, temporarily. But a maniac, no. Ever since that first delicious moment—the moment that opened up the world—everything I've done has been supremely rational. Completely logical. Absolutely necessary. And of course, I'll stop killing after tonight. I *would* be crazy to think I could keep on getting away with it.''

He scraped up a glob of salsa with a chip, stashed it, chewed loudly. I absolutely couldn't believe it. The fat slob was eating again. ''It's interesting how these things happen. It's like it was meant to be, like a portal opens and says, 'Warren, step through me.' The portal was Sadie in this case, of course.''

There was a nasty thump from the living room. Not looking up, I dumped powder into coffee, tucked away the capsule halves.

Then I pivoted in the direction of the thump, just in time to see Warren turning back, remembering me too late. He grabbed me and jerked my hair so hard I screamed.

Over his shoulder I saw what Esperanza had done—tipped the chair to which Warren had tied her. Now on the floor, chair and all, she was working at Julio's bonds with her teeth.

"Naughty girl," said Warren. "You don't know how I punish naughty girls, do you? I hurt somebody else." He gave my hair another yank.

She moved her teeth off the clothesline, but kept her head on Julio's ankles, that being the closest she could get to a hug, I supposed.

"It's going to be Rebecca this time—now, what do you think I should do with her?"

No answer.

"Rebecca! Pick that chair up."

I obeyed, righting Esperanza, giving her a little squeeze of thanks for what she'd done.

"Think about it, Esperanza." And he took me back to finish making the coffee.

Afterward, sipping it, he said to Esperanza, "You know what I'm going to do? I'm going to let you take the heat for her. That is, if you want to."

I shouted, "No, Warren Nowell, she will not! You want to hurt somebody, pick on somebody your own size."

"By all means resort to clichés, Rebecca. It'll help the situation no end. You know, we really do have a killer instinct? I'm going to give Esperanza a chance to develop hers."

"Dear God, no!"

Julio shouted, "You bastard! Leave her alone."

"You know what's in the bathroom, Esperanza?"

She shook her head.

"Something I want you to kill."

Oh, the fish. Not one of us. My heart slowed to only three times normal speed.

But Esperanza paled.

CHAPTER 21

He dropped it for a while, letting the suspense build, sipping and talking, killing cookies while Esperanza probably thought of hapless kittens and bunny rabbits hidden in the bathroom.

"I never meant to kill Sadie at all. That wasn't in the cards even for a moment. All I wanted to do was blackmail her. It all seems so stupid and petty now. I wanted her ridiculous job."

"But I thought you didn't," I said. "I thought you wanted to write a book."

"I did, of course. I do. And now I can do it. You see what I mean about things working out? I never wanted the stupid job. But Mary Ellen and Katy—and Mother, of course—were always on my back about being director. I thought I'd do them a favor, that was all." He shrugged, as if homicide were the least he could offer.

"Also, I happened to be upholding the law. You see, sweet Sadie stole the Sheffield Pearl. How, I don't know—she was probably over at Katy's one day and lifted it when Katy was drunk. Her office door was slightly open and I saw her holding it up, looking at it with this kind of dreamy smile, and then hiding it in her desk.

"I could have just called the police, but I recognized an opportunity, ladies and gentleman. I'd been hoping for one, thinking about one for so many years. A golden moment that would change my life. And finally one came to me—in the form of a glimpse of a woman looking at a pearl.'' He licked salsa from the corner of his mouth, smug as a cat.

''So I took the rest of the day and made my arrangements. Then I saw her go up on the roof with Julio. Naturally I followed and waited. I knew she'd stay there after Julio left—she treated it like her personal veranda. When he'd gone, she unhooked the plastic rope and bent down by the tank. When I came up, she said, 'Oh, Warren, look at this splendid feather boa kelp.' '' He did Sadie in falsetto.

''I whipped out the Polaroid and showed it to her.''

''The Polaroid?''

''Why, yes, Rebecca, the Polaroid. When Sadie went to the roof, I simply sneaked in and took a picture of the pearl lying in her desk drawer. Pretty incriminating, wouldn't you say? So I flashed it at her. I thought she'd try to grab it and beg for mercy, but she just seemed kind of puzzled. Finally she said, 'Warren, what's that?'

''I said, 'You know perfectly well what it is. It's the Sheffield Pearl.' '' He stowed a cookie. ''I said, 'Look, I've already called Katy. I know it's been stolen.' ''

''And then she did something unbelievably stupid. She said, 'You mean that pearl belongs to Katy Montebello?' Can you believe the nerve? The insult to my intelligence?

''I couldn't handle her garbage anymore. I told her I was prepared to call the police and also to go before the board. But of course, I let her know I'd forget the whole thing—*and* let her keep the pearl—if she'd resign. That was the whole point.

''She said obviously we couldn't go on working together. *But do you know what she meant?* Not the obvious. Not by a long shot. The bitch tried to fire me!

"I mean, can you believe that?" He paused. "I really started to get mad. Where does she get off, I'm thinking, you know what I mean? For Christ's sake, the woman's a thief. But she says, 'Listen, for what it's worth, I didn't steal that pearl. I can't tell you why I have it, but it happens to be for a legitimate reason—'

"Oh, *sure* it was. She either stole it or she received stolen property. What other choices are there?"

We were silent with our own guilty knowledge.

"The bitch had the gall to say, 'I'm sorry it has to end this way,' and she started to leave. Then she turned back around and she said, 'Warren, I'm going to tell you something. I'm really going to go out on a limb, and I hope I don't hurt your feelings. Please believe me when I tell you that I know this isn't your fault, I understand that. I've felt terrible for you ever since I met your mother.'

"Now you see where this is leading. The bitch! My mother! I just started to see red. I said, 'Where the hell did you meet my mother?'

"She said, 'Katy brought her around to some event or other. I've met her several times, actually.' She put a hand on my wrist, *can you believe it*?" One after another, fat hands moving like motors, he stuffed cookies and chomped, giving new meaning to the term "fast and furious."

"Can you believe she touched me? In the very act of insulting my mother? She said, 'Warren, nobody should have to go through what you went through.' Do you *believe* it? She didn't even know my mother! She said, 'You don't have to live with this, really you don't—you can get better.' " He was doing the falsetto again.

"And that was it. After that, nothing but red rage."

I said, "That was it? You mean you don't remember what happened next?"

"Of course I remember. I meant that was it for her. What

happened was, I slammed her up against the wall of the lab and tried like hell to choke her to death. But the bitch got away and jumped in the tank. She knew I can't swim.

"But by then the portal had opened. Sure, it was the rage that made me slam her and try to choke her, but when I had my hands around her neck, something else kicked in, you know that? Something I wanted all my life and didn't know how to get. Know what that was, my captive audience?"

Even I couldn't speak by this point.

"Power. I finally felt power, came into my own power. I never knew what that felt like before. She was in the tank, scared to death. . . . You should have seen the look on her face. Warren Nowell had the power of life and death over Sadie Swedlow, and she knew it. Can you imagine what an exhilarating moment that was? I was really enjoying myself by this time. That's what I meant about the killer instinct. We really do have one, you understand? We really have one. And mine had just kicked in.

"She tried to scream, but she couldn't. At least I think that's what she was trying to do; she kept looking like she was trying to make sounds come out, but maybe I damaged her vocal cords or something. When she finally spoke, she whispered. She said, 'Warren,' in this little whispery, pleading way, and I knew exactly what to do. Apologize. I said, 'Omigod, Sadie, I don't know what came over me,' and garbage like that, all the time taking off my coat and rolling up my sleeves. And I could tell she trusted me again. All those months of knowing one guy, it's pretty hard to see him as another guy, I guess. She couldn't know what had just happened to me—all she thought was, I got out of control and then I went back to normal.

"The bottom line is, she let me try to help her out of the tank."

I spoke quickly to stop him going into the details. "You drowned her."

He nodded. "I drowned her. And then I tied her arm to the fence to hold her still while I got Marty's jacket and letter opener, and you know the rest. Except for one thing—I put the pearl in Sadie's hand and closed it. I thought I had it rigged so the hand wouldn't open.

"I thought the police theory would be that one of them stole it, the other found out, and they fought over it, but—" he paused, waxing philosophical "—it wasn't to be. Anyway, all that, of course, was before I remembered Katy knew I knew about it. So I had to kill her, too."

"But I don't see why you needed to get the pearl."

"Because Katy might have told someone I called. And if it were ever found in the tank, that someone just might remember. Now, of course, I can simply put it back in her house—I'll get my mother to take me there on some pretext—and if anyone ever says anything, I'll say they must be mistaken. I'm sure you see the problem—I can't simply go on killing people at random on the off chance she might have told them. Though I don't know about that maid of hers—"

He was going to kill her, I knew it then. He was going to kill us and he was going to kill her next, and then he'd starting killing people at random, women, probably, and maybe he'd finally kill his mother and then call the cops the way Edmund Emil Kemper had done. Kemper, who was now doing a life sentence, had racked up ten victims, including his grandparents, before he'd worked up the courage to murder the one he was really mad at. And when he finally killed her, he took out another woman as well, bringing his total to twelve. But murder, apparently, wasn't the whole point: he ground up his mother's larynx in the garbage disposal.

I don't know why Kemper popped into my mind—

maybe what Warren had said about not killing people at random. The way he said it belied the words. And then when he mentioned Yolie, I knew. I knew that I could blurt out that she didn't know, that I knew she didn't know, and it wouldn't save her—he might even use my words as his rationalization.

Warren yawned. Was the Seconal starting to work? He released Esperanza and then me, using me for his hostage. He took us into the bathroom and gave her the spear gun, making very sure to keep my body between his and the weapon.

Despite old sayings about shooting fish in a barrel, puffers aren't that big, and Esperanza missed the first time. Warren slapped me a couple of times to improve her aim.

The second time, by placing the point of the spear nearly on her fish, she got one, and it nearly broke my heart that he wouldn't let me gather her up when she sat down and cried in the middle of the bathroom floor.

But there was a bright side. Warren was so annoyed at the damage caused by the spear, he let her net the second.

I was encouraged by the yawn. When I retied Esperanza, I not only didn't tie her tightly, I barely tied her at all. He didn't check the knots.

"I need more coffee."

Delighted to oblige. I slipped in the third cap.

He sipped and watched me contentedly while I put together a perfectly splendid fish stew.

I filleted the fish, finding the prized liver and guts, then chopped onions, garlic, and tomatoes, just as he predicted, biding my time. He was big and he'd eaten a lot. It would take time, but three caps of the stuff would work eventually. I kept telling myself that. Over and over.

The stew was simmering in a pot, the skillet I'd used for

sautéeing still on the stove, Warren sitting on the counter when he began to yawn and blink steadily.

Julio said, "You'll never get away with it, Warren. What the hell do you plan to do with four bodies?"

"Why, nothing." He showed us his tonsils, didn't even stifle the yawn. "You and Rebecca simply made puffer bouillabaisse, and poisoned yourselves and two kids. The reason will never be known." He shrugged, smiling. He rubbed an eye with his gun hand. The bastard was having the time of his life.

Never even turning my head, taking aim out of the corner of my eye, I picked up the skillet with both hands and bashed the hand holding the gun, still at his face. I swung the hot pan like a baseball bat, swung my whole body with it, hoping to injure both hand and face. The gun flew out of his hand, over the counter, dropping on the other side in the living room.

He could have gone for me, subdued me, and then retrieved the gun, but he was too woozy, perhaps, and I still had the frying pan. Instead, he went for the gun, swinging his legs around and over the counter, dropping off the other side.

It was a smart move. I either had to climb up and drop down to follow him, or go around the counter and into the living room through the door. I chose that way, and by the time I got there, he was picking himself up, now holding the gun, but he hadn't yet had the time to wheel around.

"Warren, look out!" Esperanza's voice was desperate.

He stared at her, and caught a hagfish in the face. Slime hung on him like cobwebs. "Aaaarrrh!"

Automatically his hand rose to wipe off the loathsome mess, and Esperanza threw another. He threw up the other hand to defend himself. And I crowned him with the skillet.

He fell forward. I hit him again, and then a third time, prostrating him. When he was lying on his nose, I hit him again.

"Rebecca?" Esperanza's voice was small. "Do you want the gun?"

She was holding it with two hands the way she'd seen the good guys do it on television.

CHAPTER 22

"It's easy to catch a hagfish. They can't see you coming because they don't have eyes."

"Gross." But Keil was jealous, I could tell.

"Okay," said Libby. "If it's so easy, let's see you do it again. Bet you five dollars you won't do it again.'

Esperanza's golden face lit up. "Bet I will."

Marty said, "Do we have to? At the dinner table? Couldn't we talk about something else?"

Libby and Esperanza spoke as one, outraged. "But we have to! It's our therapy."

"Just not hagfish, okay? The frying pan, sure; shooting the puffer, no big deal, just no hagfish. Please?"

Keil stuffed turkey and dressing into his mouth, but Marty took a break, held her napkin over her mouth for quite a while, finally swallowed, and resumed eating. Slowly.

It was Thanksgiving, and we were all together—all the Whiteheads, even Don; both the Sotos; me, of course; and Ricky. It was our reunion, for all of us who'd been through it, except Ava.

The kids had been rushed into therapy, and from the way Marty was behaving, I thought maybe she'd enrolled herself as well. From her refusal to invite Ava, for one thing. "I'm sick and tired of being a victim. I don't care if she cries all day and all night. She makes the kids miserable, she makes me miserable, and if we ask her to step back, stop trying to

222

control us, she turns into a martyr and makes *us* the bad
guys. We all end up feeling manipulated, and for once, we're
going to think about ourselves first.''

I thought that had the ring of a few fifty-minute hours to
it. Also, the way she'd started taking care of the kids, staying
home, doing things with them, bespoke a different attitude.
But maybe she wasn't in therapy—maybe the sight of Libby's
swollen wrists and ankles, the horror of knowing she'd nearly
lost her, the weeks and weeks of screaming, sweating nightmares, had simply wrought a change. They say people who
go through an ordeal often undergo a spiritual experience.
Such a thing was hard to imagine where Marty was concerned, but watching her actually behaving like a mother,
being civil to Don, seemingly enjoying so humble a thing as
a holiday with family and friends, no payoff expected, was a
pretty strong argument.

Another was that she'd been offered the job as director and
had turned it down, saying she wanted to spend more time
with her kids. Who knew? Anything was possible. We'd been
together a lot since August and I'd enjoyed her, thought the
true Marty—not the female Sammy Glick—might be coming
into its own.

She wasn't dating anyone at the moment, and neither was
Don, but neither of them talked in terms of getting back
together. That was a romance that had never been one to
begin with, and it seemed good and over. He'd been invited
to dinner because the kids wanted him.

And Ricky was there because Amber was spending the
holiday with her mother. He seemed a little morose, and was
having a little wine, but he swore he'd really cut down on his
drinking. Libby had told me Amber told her he was in AA,
but he seemed not to be in it with both feet. Still, Libby said,
Amber was keeping her fingers crossed. Maybe he'd come
through for her one day.

As for Julio and me, we were an item. Rob was the first

to tell me. He knew because an unfortunate thing had occurred. The day after the ordeal, when everything was still shaking down, a TV crew caught us leaving the police station, Julio's arm around my shoulder, mine around Esperanza's. Rob had seen it in Cambridge. He said we looked like a family.

We weren't that, but we'd grown very close in three months. Libby and Esperanza had dreams of me dying, Julio dying, everyone in their family dying. Part of their therapy was for me to spend a lot of time with them. So I came to Monterey a lot. Esperanza was spending the school year with Julio instead of her mother. She'd gone back to Santa Barbara for a while, but the nightmares had come every night, and every day she'd cry until her mother let her call Julio to make sure he was still alive. Finally she admitted she wanted to be there for a while.

So Julio moved out of the house with the awful memories and into a much nicer, sunnier one, warm with new furniture, new rugs, new curtains that I'd helped him pick out.

But we'd by no means moved from two days of fun and games with Warren back to our peaceful and tranquil lives. First of all, there was one more tragedy to be gotten through: Mary Ellen's body was found at Warren's home after his arrest. He'd apparently dispatched her before coming to work that fine Monday morning.

And then there were the nightmares—not just for the kids, but for us all. And in our waking hours there was reliving our story, retelling it. People who go through something terrible have to do that, repeatedly, till they've healed themselves. Something in the neighborhood of sixty times, I'm told. That was why we'd made a special effort to spend Thanksgiving together and why Marty was trying not to throw up while we talked slime.

"Esperanza, you're hardly eating a bite."

Libby said, "Oh, Mom, you sound like Grandma."

"Sorry."

I suspected Marty could care less whether Esperanza ate. Her problem was that Esperanza was talking. She was desperately trying to stop her.

"Well, see, I got the idea when I realized I was going to be able to get free. I was thinking about how I could really hurt him and I knew. It just came to me, like a message from God."

Keil said, "There's no such thing as God."

"You know how much slime those things can make? My dad showed me once when he was trying to convince me I should like them. It's, like, ten times their weight. Twenty times. It's like—out of some horror movie. There's no way that much gunk could come out of such a little wormy thing."

"Chill out, will you?" Keil was furious he hadn't gone through the great adventure with us. "Everybody's already heard what a hero you were. About a hundred and nine times."

"Ricky hasn't!"

"Keil," I said, "there's something I never got a chance to ask you. I chased somebody in the warehouse the day after Sadie was killed. That was you, wasn't it?"

"What makes you think that?"

"You had access to a key—your mom's, or maybe Ricky's that you got from Amber. You're about the right height and build. And you got a phone call that sounded like a job a few minutes before I left the house."

He looked very smug, very pleased himself. "Trap Door's clientele is strictly confidential."

"Oh, *sure*," said Esperanza. "Like attorney-client privilege, right, Rebecca? *Mr.* Important."

She sounded like a brat. I knew there could be only one explanation—she was getting a crush on him.

I said, "Okay, you don't have to tell me. But let me guess, okay? Humor me."

He shrugged.

"The client's name started with 'A.' "

Libby took up the game. "Amber!"

"And she wanted you to recover a certain piece of property for her."

"The pearl!" Both girls were into the spirit now. Maybe I'd successfully changed the subject.

"I was kind of wondering how much you charge for a job like that."

"Confidential."

"Ha. I know! That's why she gave you her Swiss army knife." Libby preened herself over her deduction.

Ricky started. "Santa Claus brought her that knife."

"Oh, Ricky, who believes in Santa Claus? Don't you want to know what it feels like to pick one of them up?"

"Don't they wiggle?"

"Oh, *wiggle*. Wiggle! It's like having a whole handful of snakes at once. And they're so slimy, the only way you can keep hold of them is to squeeze real tight, but then they might pop right through your hands. So you've got to hold them in both hands, and you've got to be *real* quick—"

"Hey, Mom," asked Keil, "what's for dessert?"

About the Author

Julie Smith is the author of many mysteries, including *New Orleans Mourning*, winner of the 1990 Edgar Allen Poe Award for Best Mystery Novel. A former reporter for *The New Orleans Times-Picayune*, the author lived for a long time in San Francisco and currently makes her home in Santa Barbara, California.